Unfolded

UNFOLDED

Copyright © 2022 by Emily Walsh

First paperback edition April 2018

Book design by Emily Walsh

ISBN 9798841363347 (paperback)
ISBN 9798844068607 (hardcover)

Diary Entry

26/8/15

Willow

I decided to come to the forest today. It's what I usually do when I'm bored. Sometimes I walk around and look at pretty stones to take home. And other times I just sit on a rock and stare into the lake, that's close enough to what I'm doing now.

I was texting my cousin Jade earlier. She was supposed to be here with me. She hasn't showed up yet.

Oh! My art teacher, Ms Parker is on the other side of the lake. I'm going to go and hide until she leaves.

Ok, she's gone. I'm going to go back to the rock I was sitting on.

Hey you know when you get a feeling that you're not actually alone when you think you are? I'm having one of those moments right now. I know I'm probably just overreacting about it but I wanted to write it down. I tend to write a lot of things in my journal. I could've sworn someone just tapped me on the shoulder, but I looked back and nobody was there. I think I'm going to go home now. This is getting really weird out

here. Wait I think I saw

One

Ivy

'It just stops right there,' I say, almost in a whisper
'I know, I wonder what she actually saw,' Holly replies.
'Yeah, it was the day she died. So it's definitely
evidence. She was probably writing and then whoever
killed her just did it then and there so she couldn't write

anymore,' Holly suggests. 'Or she could have been in shock and stopped writing after what she saw,'.

'If she was just in shock she wouldn't have written *wait I just saw a*, she would have just stopped writing straight after what she saw,' I correct.

'That makes more sense,'

I flip through Willow's journal again just to make sure that she didn't write anything else that could possibly be hints to what happened to her that day.

'Ivy I don't think we need to flip through anymore we've already done that so many times now,'

'I know, I'm just checking,'

'Ivy!'.

'One minute Holly my mum's calling me,'.

'Ok!'

   I run down the stairs, almost skipping a step, and enter the kitchen.

'Hi mum. What's wrong?'

'Hi Ivy, you and Holly are trying that closed case from a few years back right? What was her name? Willow Evans?' My mother asks.

'Yes why?'

'I thought it might be helpful if you went to her cousin's house, she was apparently close with her, I'm sure she could tell you something about her that might help,' She suggests.

'Yeah, that's a good idea. I'll tell Holly about it and see what she thinks,'.

'Alright Ivy,'.

'Bye mum,'.

'Bye!' my mum calls.'

I run back up the stairs being more careful this time so I don't nearly skip a step again, and go into my bedroom to Holly.

'My mum gave me an idea!' I tell her.

'Oh, what is it?' Holly asks me.

'She said we should go to her cousins house, and that Willow was close with her

cousin, so she could probably tell us something helpful,' I explain.

'That's a good idea. When are you free to go?'.

'I can go anytime you're free,' I say.

'Ok! Tomorrow after school?' She asks.

'Yeah alright. I'll meet you outside of the school gate and we can go straight from there,' I tell her.

'Ok, see you tomorrow Ivy,' Holly says while grabbing her bag and coat and walking towards the door.

'Bye!' I say as I watch her leave my room.

I'm actually really excited for tomorrow. I wonder if we'll get any information. Maybe we'll learn some things about Willow. Holly's going to want to be friends with her. Holly's always looking for new friends. She makes a new friend and then she ignores them after a week. She only has two *real* friends. Lucas and I. Lucas is our other best friend. Holly has known Lucas since they were really small. No, I'm going to interview her and that's it, nothing more. But maybe she'll ask me to be friends. But she's going to have to be serious, if we want to solve this murder she's going to have to stay focoused on the plan. And Holly making a new friend is *not* part of the plan. But maybe if I let Holly get close with her I can find out more about Willow and then it could possibly be easier to solve the case. I'll talk to Holly at school tomorrow, I hope she doesn't want to be her friend. I *need* to stop thinking about this.

•••

I'm standing outside of the school gate waiting for Holly to come out of the school building.
'Hey Ivy, sorry my locker was stuck. I couldn't get it open,' Holly says while grabbing my arm and practically dragging me to the crossing.
'Hi,' I say.
Holly's the more outgoing one of the two of us, I'm quieter and don't talk to many people. Holly and Lucas are my only friends. That's why I get so excited about meeting someone new. Holly makes friends so easily. I don't know how she does it.

'Hey! Ivy! Are you there?' Holly says waving a hand in front of my face.

'Oh, sorry. I was just-'

'Daydreaming. I know,' she finishes my sentence for me, ' Where's the house?' she asks.

'Uhm... I don't know. I'll text my mum,' I tell her.

'Ok! Are you excited?' Holly asks. 'I am! I wonder if Willow's cousin will want to be friends with us! Ok Ivy. I know you're not great at talking to people, and I know you're the more responsible, serious friend. But just hear me out ok? Imagine. You and I, friends with the dead popular girl's closest cousin! Wouldn't it be great? Think of all of the people that would-'

'Holly- Please. Take this seriously. I will be friends with her under certain circumstances. We will only be friends with her to become close with her so we can get information out of her. Not to be more *popular*. It's not like *you* need any more friends, you've made more friends in the past two weeks than I have in my whole life! Anyways, Willow wasn't even popular. People only know her name because she's *missing*. We don't know if she's dead or alive, so maybe you shouldn't call her *the dead popular girl*,'.

'Ok, we'll be friends with her to get information. Not to be popular,' She agrees.

'Good,' I say, not really knowing what I mean by *good*.

'Oh my mum texted me back,' I say while entering my password, to get into my phone. 'She said it's house fourteen on Oakley Drive,'

'Ok, put it on your maps.' Holly tells me.

'It's fine I know where that is,' I tell her.

'Are you sure Ivy?'

'I'm sure,'

We continue walking down the road until we see the sign, *OAKLEY DRIVE*.

We walk onto the street, not too sure where we're going anymore.

'Ok. Let's look at the first house on the left. So that's number ten. Maybe this way. No wait, that's nine. Go the other way,' I say as we turn around to go in the direction.

'Here's eleven, so keep going this way,' Holly tells me. We walk up farther until we see houses thirteen and fourteen.

'Ok, here it is,' I say, as we take a step towards the house.

'Let's go,' Holly says excitedly.

Two

Holly

We step up to the front door of the house. I lift my arm hesitantly and knock on the door. I hear footsteps coming towards the door. Suddenly a girl opens the door.

The girl has dark green hair and she's wearing a black t-shirt with a black and white, striped, long-sleeve shirt under it. She's also wearing a black pleated skirt with ripped tights.

'Hi,' I say. 'Are you Jade Evans? Willow's cousin?' Ivy asks.

She looks so nervous. She should have just let me do the talking.

'Yes, I am. Hi. Who are you?' Jade asks politely. Jade seems confused. I guess the case was closed four years ago, so she probably hasn't been questioned in around three years. The case was closed in 2016, because the police couldn't find any clues on what had happened to Willow.

'I'm Ivy Jones. My friend Holly and I would like to ask you a few questions. If that's ok with you,' Ivy asks Jade, still looking extremely nervous. Ivy hates talking to people. But she's been desperate to solve this case herself ever since it was closed. And now she's finally decided to do it.

'Yes, of course come in,' Jade smiles, inviting us in.

We enter the house. It's really nice inside.

'Ok, sit down here,' Jade says, gesturing towards the kitchen chairs. Ivy and I sit down. Ivy hangs her school bag on the back of her chair. She looks so serious. I get why, but she looks as if she's a real detective.

'So, Jade. You don't mind if I record the conversation do you?' Ivy asks.

'No, I don't mind. Do whatever you need to!' Jade tells her.

Jade seems really nice. I want to be friends with her, really badly. And not to just get information out of her. I want to be friends with her to actually be *real* friends. I hope she's going to be this nice every time we see her! Ok I need to actually start taking this seriously, or i'll be the one dead in the lake next, because Ivy would have murdered me for not treating this like a *real* case.

Ivy and I were thirteen when Willow was found dead. We both love watching true crime documentaries on the television. And when we were twelve, we bought a fake case to solve online and tried to solve it on a sleepover. We actually did it. We kept buying more of them, because they were so fun to solve together. We were only twelve, solving fake murder cases. So now Ivy thinks it's about time we try and solve a *real* case together.

Ivy

I turn around in my seat and reach back for my school bag.
I open my bag and take out my phone.
'Just a second now,' I tell Jade and Holly, as I press down on
the power button on my phone.

Once my phone turns on, I type my password and go
straight to the *Voice Recorder* app.
'I'm about to start recording,' I say. I press the *record* button.

•••

Transcript

Ivy: Jade, you're Willow Evans' cousin
right?

Jade: Yes, I am.

Ivy: Describe your relationship with Willow
please.

Jade: Ok. Willow was my cousin. We were very
close. We knew everything about each other.

Ivy: Would you mind sharing some things about Willow please?

Jade: Yes, of course. Willow used to go to the forest near her house when she was bored. She went there the day she died. You've probably read her diary entry from that day. So Willow was most likely murdered in the forest that day. I have a feeling that the killer is someone she knew. Someone we all know. What I mean by *someone we all know* is me, you, and Holly.

Ivy: So you think someone *I* know murdered Willow?

Jade: Yes.

Ivy: Do you have any other information about Willow that could be useful?

Jade: No.

Ivy: Are you sure?

Jade: I'm sure.

Ivy: Ok. Did you see Willow that day?

Jade: No.

Ivy: Did you have any contact with Willow
the day she went
    missing?

Jade: No.

Ivy: I would recommend it if you *didn't* lie
to me.

Jade: I'm not *lying* to you, Ivy.

Ivy: Yes, you are. Holly and I were reading
the entry Willow
    wrote the day Willow disappeared.

Jade: Oh- The entry…

Ivy: Don't lie to me. You won't get away
with it.

Jade: Ok.

Ivy: I think we're done here.

Jade: Ok.

•••

    I press *end* on my phone. I don't think I've held a
conversation for that long with someone other than Holly or
my mum.

'Alright, Holly and I are going to go home now. Thank you so
much for your time,' I say to Jade, getting up from my seat.

'Ok!' Jade says, also getting up.

'Bye! I hope to see you again,' Holly squeals, leaving her chair
and making her way to the door.

    We leave the house and begin to walk back to our houses.

'That was so pointless,' I say. 'She didn't give us anything
useful. I already know everything she told us,' I continue.

'I thought she was nice,' Holly protests.

'She was completely useless, she only told us what we have
already read in her journal,'

'I know, but she's still nice!'

'Of course you think she's nice. You think everyone's nice,' I
remark.

We continue walking, in silence.

I'm kind of suspicious of Jade, she was being *way* too nice to us. And she didn't tell us much. I feel like she's definitely hiding something.

I know some things about this case so far. I know where Willow lived, her closest friends, her favourite things to do, the day she went missing, and the day she was found. I need a lot more information than that to solve it though. This is a lot different to solving one of those fake cases I bought online. I wasn't expecting it to be easy or anything but this is *really* hard. I don't have any idea what to do first. I've read lots of murder books, so I should know what to do first. I'll just keep doing more research and think of someone else to interview. But first I'm going to add Jade to the *persons of interest* list.

I might interview some of Willows' teachers. I know she was quite close with the art teacher Ms. Parker. So I could stay after school tomorrow and talk to her. And I might talk to her science teacher too. I know from reading some of her diary entries that she doesn't like science, but I'll just try anyway.

I turn on my computer and go to google. I type *how to solve a murder case* and click enter. I go to the first website that I see. I scroll down the page scanning it with my eyes in case I find something important.

I was looking on different websites for around two hours so I close my laptop and sit on my bed. How am I supposed to solve this case if Holly won't take it seriously? She's supposed to be helping me with this.

I pick up my phone and dial Holly's number.

'Hello?' she says.

'Hey Holly, it's Ivy,'.

'Oh hi! Did you find any tips on how we can solve this?'.

'Nothing,' I tell her.

'Oh well, we will solve it in the end! I know we will, Ivy. Don't underestimate yourself, you're capable of doing whatever you want,' Holly tells me, encouragingly. She's sort of acting as if I'm the only one doing this. I don't dare mention it to her though, I don't want to start any drama before we even get anywhere with this.

'Holly,' I say. 'I didn't find anything online, but I did think of an idea myself,'

'What is it?',

'We could interview some teachers Willow was close with. I haven't found anything that tells me they have been interviewed already, so I thought we could talk to them tomorrow after school,'

'Yeah, ok! Great idea. I'll see you tomorrow, bye Ivy,'

'Bye Holly,' I say, hanging up the phone, and dropping it onto my bedsheets.

'Ivy!' Holly calls, running over to me.

'Hi, Holly. Are you ready?' I ask.

'Yeah. Let's go,' we start walking towards the art classroom.

I knock on the door, and hesitantly opened the door.

'Oh hello girls, is everything ok?' Ms. Parker asks.

'Hi!' Holly says excitedly.

'We would like to ask you a few questions, if that's ok with you?'

'Yes, of course! Take a seat.' We sit down at a desk beside her.

'Ok, do you mind if I record the conversation?' I ask, taking my phone out from my blazer pocket.

'I don't mind. What's this about?' She asks, tapping her pen on her desk.

'It's about the alleged murder of Willow Evans,' I tell her.

'Oh, ok then. Start whenever you're ready,'.

I press the record button.

'Were you with Willow the day she disappeared?'.

'Yes, I was. She had a class with me earlier that day,'.

'Do you-'.

'I have a question!!,' Holly interrupts.

'*Holly!*' I snap. 'Don't cut me off. I'm sorry. Do you know anything about what happened the day Willow went missing?'.

'I was going for a walk that day, after school finished. I was in a forest, and I saw a girl. She had black hair, and she was wearing a green hoodie. Willow was wearing a green hoodie earlier that day. I think I saw Willow Evans in the forest, but it could have been anyone.' Ms Parker tells me. She looks scared, I'm becoming suspicious of what she could have done to Willow.

'Did you murder Willow?' Holly asks.

'What? No!' Ms Parker gasps. 'If you're going to ask me if I *murdered* my student, I would like you to please leave my classroom,'

'*Holly!*' I snap. 'I am so sorry, Ms Parker. Holly doesn't know what she's saying. We'll be leaving now. Come on Holly. Thank you Ms Parker, I'll be back soon by *myself* if that's ok with you?'

'Yes, that's fine with me. I'm not a suspect... am I?' *Oh God.* She thinks we're *suspecting* her now.

'No, you're not a suspect. I don't believe you would ever hurt a student,' I lie. I am suspecting her right now. I can't help myself but wonder: *Did Ms Parker murder Willow Evans?*

•••

I walk into my bedroom, lock the door, sit at my desk, pull out my laptop, and start typing out the transcript.

I finally finish writing the transcript, so i flip back a couple of pages to my *persons of interest* list

Persons Of Interest

Jade Evans

Angela Parker

    I close my journal and put it back in the same spot where I had picked it up from. I get up from my chair, and start walking towards my bedroom door. I open my door and start walking downstairs.

    I walk into the sitting room.

'Hi mum, hi dad,' I close the sitting room door, and walk to the bookshelf.

'Hi,' My dad says. 'Are you looking for something?' he asks.

'Yes, is there a book on solving a case?'

'No not in this house Ivy,' He tells me, getting up from the sofa and walking out of the sitting room, and into the kitchen.

'Ok, thanks. I'll be on my way to the bookshop. Text me if you need me,' I take one last glance at the shelf and walk over to the door.

'Alright, Ivy,' I slip my shoes on and grab the door handle.

'Ivy?' my mum calls.

'Yes?'

'Do you have a jacket? It's cold,'

'I'll get one now,' I run up the stairs, into my bedroom, and grab my coat from my bed.

  'Where are you going Ivy?' My older sister Alice asks.

'To the bookshop, I'm looking for books on solving cases. Want to come?'

'Ok!' Alice runs to her room to get her bag and coat.

We walk down the stairs and leave.

  'So, you're trying to solve Willow Evan's murder?' Alice asks.

'*Alleged* murder. And yes, Holly and I are trying to solve it together,' I correct.

'Oh come on Ivy, everyone knows she was murdered,'

'I don't know, Alice. For all we know she could have just wrote that entry to make it seem like she was murdered. Maybe she left the forest and went somewhere else. Somewhere nobody would suspect she'd go, and jumped into a lake. She could've drowned. She could have gotten lost and just died. We'll never know, unless Holly and I are successful,' I love coming up with theories to unsolved cases.

'I guess,'

 We walk into our local bookshop. I immediately run off to the *crime* section to look.

 After not being able to find anything, I walk up to the help desk.

'Hello,' I say friendly.

'Hello dear,' the old lady at the desk says. 'What can I help you with?'.

'I was wondering if you had any books on solving a murder case? A friend and I are trying to solve one,'.

'I'll have a look for you dear,'. She starts typing aggressively. She looks up and says 'I do. I'll get it now for you,'.

'Thank you,'. The old lady gets up and makes her way to the *crime* section. I stand at the help desk, waiting.

 She gets back and hands me the book.

'Here you are. Good luck solving the case,' she says.

'Thank you so much,' I smile, walking away.

•••

 Alice and I walk back into the house.

'Are you back already girls?' Mum asks.

'Yeah, I found a book. I'm going to go upstairs and start reading it,' I say. I walk up the stairs, Alice behind me.

 I walk into my room, and lock the door. I toss the book onto my bed. I sit down on my bed and pick up the book. I start reading.

Three

Holly

I'm standing in the hallway, waiting for Ivy to get out of her
class. I see Lucas, another friend of Ivy and I.
'Hey Holly,' Lucas says. 'Where's Ivy?'.

'She's in a class, I'm waiting for her to come out,' I say, turning to look behind me. Ivy is walking down the hallway with a closed book in her hands, her bag on her back, and her earphones in her ears.

'She's pretty, isn't she,' Lucas says, admiring Ivy.

'Shut *up* Lucas, she's my best friend!' I joke, as Ivy takes out her earphones and stands with us.

'Hi,' She says, putting her earphones in her bag.

'Hi, Ivy,' Lucas says, staring at the floor.

'Hello,' I say.

'So... what are we doing?' She asks.

'We could go to the café?' I suggest. 'The three of us,'.

'Ok!' Ivy says, tossing her bag back on her shoulders.

'Alright,' Lucas glances at Ivy, and back to the ground.

'I can't believe it's finally the end of the school year!' I say.

'Yeah. We can do stuff all the time now without school or homework being an issue,' Lucas replies.

'Not for me. I have to mind my little sister. The girl is a pain in the ass,' I sigh.

'Oh stop, Holly. She's only like what? Five?' Ivy says.

'Six,' I correct.

'I was close enough,'.

I have a little sister named Harper. She's a lot younger than me. I'm sixteen and she's six. My parents really have a thing going on. Holly, Harper. We both have a *H* at the start of our names. And as I said I'm sixteen and she's six. It'll always be that way. I'll be seventeen next year and Harper will be seven. You see what I mean?

•••

We sit down at an empty table. Ivy takes her laptop out of her bag and opens it.

'Has Ivy mentioned we're trying to solve the Willow Evans case?' I ask Lucas.

'No, I haven't been talking to her,' He says, nervously.

'One minute I'm going to the bathroom, I'll be back,' I tell Ivy and Lucas. I honestly just want to see if Lucas says anything to Ivy. He clearly likes her.

Ivy shoots me an annoyed look as I leave the table.

Ivy

'Ivy?' Lucas asks, running a hand through his hair.

'Yeah?' I look at him.

'Do you want to get coffee?'

'Alright,' I say, getting up from my chair. I walk up to the counter, Lucas following behind me.

I order a coffee each, for myself, Lucas, and Holly. I stand and wait.

'Ivy?' Lucas says again.

'Yes?' I say, annoyed. But trying to sound polite.

'I'll pay,'

'Are you sure?'

'I'm sure,'

I don't say anything else.

The girl at the counter hands me the drinks. I take two, mine and Holly's. Lucas takes his own. We walk back to the table and sit down.

'I'm back!' Holly says, sliding back into her chair.

'Hi,' Lucas mumbles.

'Ivy? Lucas?' Holly asks. 'Do you have something to tell me?'.

'No... why?' I say, confused.

'Oh,' Holly looks disappointed.

'Holly, I'm not dating Lucas,' I say, annoyed. 'I'm not dating *anyone*, and I don't plan to either,'.

'Oh, I thought you liked Lucas,' Holly says.

'*No* Holly, he's my friend! I don't plan on dating one of my best friends,' I look over at Lucas, he looks upset. *Oh My God. He doesn't like me, does he?*

'I'll be back in a minute,' I tell them, getting up from my seat. I close my laptop and put it back into my bag, and run to the bathroom.

I'm going to *kill* Holly. Not literally, but she's being annoying. She knows I don't like Lucas. *God.* Lucas is my best friend.

I walk out of the bathroom.

35

I sit back down at the table.

'You guys going to the party tonight?' Holly asks.

'I don't know Holly... I might just stay home and study,' I say.

'Oh come *on,* Ivy. You never come to parties!' She complains.

'Ivy, come. *Please*! Just this once,' Lucas pleads.

'*Fine,*' I say. 'Just this once,'.

'*Yes!*' Holly squeals.

I walk into my house. *I really don't want to go to that party tonight.*

'Hi, Ivy,' Alice says. 'You coming later?'.

'Yeah, Holly and Lucas practically *begged* me to,'.

'It'll be fun! Come upstairs, we need to find you a dress,' Alice grabs my hand and starts running up the stairs. I almost fell trying to keep up with her.

We go to Alice's room.

'I'll have a look in here. You wait on my bed,' she orders. I walk to her bed, and sit down. Alice never lets me in here.

'I have the *perfect* dress for you!' Alice runs out of her walk-in-wardrobe, and hands me a sage green floral dress.

'Alice—'

'Ivy! Just try it on, it'll look nice!'

'Fine,' I say. I walk to the bathroom.

I take off my uniform, and put on the dress. I hate wearing dresses. That's more Holly's thing. Holly always goes to school parties. She's popular. Everyone knows her. I'm the complete opposite of Holly. I prefer to stay home and read, or study. Lucas usually goes to parties too, I'm the one who doesn't do things like that.

I stare into the mirror. I hate the dress. It looks ridiculous. I don't want to go. I walk out of the bathroom and back to Alice's room.

'The dress looks *amazing*, Ivy!' Alice stands up.

'I don't think it—'

'I don't want to hear it,' she cuts me off. 'It looks perfect. Now I'm going to do your makeup!'

'No.' I say. 'No. You're already making me wear a *dress*. You are *absolutely not* doing my makeup,'.

'Oh, Ivy. Just let me try!'

'No, Alice. You're going to make it all *sparkly,*'.

' I promise I won't, Ivy. Just *please* let me try,' she pleads. I do wear makeup. It's just... Alice and I are so different. She does sparkly, glittery, bright makeup when she goes out. I don't wear bright colours, or glittery eyeshadow. I don't even *wear* eyeshadow.

'Come on, Ivy!' She's starting to convince me now.

'Fine,'.

'*Yes!*' She takes my hand and we walk over to her dressing table.

'Sit down please,' I sit. Alice starts to do my makeup.

'Ok, one last thing, and then we're done,' Alice picks up a brush and puts blush on it. 'Done!' she puts the brush down. 'Finally,' I'm about to get up when Alice stops me. 'Hair is next,' Alice picks up a hairbrush and a hair straightener.

Alice begins to brush out my hair. She uses the straightener to curl it. I don't know how people use a hair straightener to *curl* their hair.

'How much longer is this going to take?' I ask.

'Not much longer. I only have a little bit of hair left,' she continues to curl my hair.

'Done!' she puts down the straightener. 'Do you like it?'.

'It's nice,' I say. I'm not lying, I do like it.

Four

Ivy

We walk up to the door of the house where the party's being
held. Holly reaches to
open the door, when I stop her.
'Holly!' I grab her arm. 'Are you supposed to just walk in?'.

'Yes, Ivy. You just walk in,' Holly sighs.

'Ok, just making sure,'.

Holly opens the door, and we step inside.

'There's so many people!' I say, over the sound of the music blasting, and people shouting.

'Well,' Holly says. 'That's the whole point of a party,'. We walk further in, and Lucas closes the door. Alice runs off to her friends.

'I wonder if any of Willow's friends from when she was still alive are here?' I say.

'Ivy, we don't need to be thinking about the case right now. Just have fun!' Holly shouts, over the noise.

We walk into the living room. There are people everywhere. Holly runs over to the radio. She changes the song, and starts dancing.

I grab Lucas' hand and drag him out of the sitting room.

'What are we doing Ivy?' he asks.

'Looking for Willow's friends,'.

We walk around the house for a bit, but we don't see anyone who used to be friends with Willow yet.

I hear a phone ringing. Lucas walks over and picks it up.

'Ivy?' he asks. They're looking for you or Holly,' Lucas hands the phone to me, and I put it to my ear.

'Hello?'.

Silence

'Is anyone there?'.

Silence

'Ok, what kind of joke is this Lucas?' I snap.

'Ivy,' he says. 'I'm not joking. Someone asked for you, or
Holly. Their exact words were 'let *me speak to Ivy, or Holly*,'.

'Lucas... no one's on the other e—'.

Gunshot

'Lucas,' I dropped the phone and backed away. 'I heard a
gunshot,'.

'What?'.

'You heard me, Lucas. I heard a *gunshot*,'.

'Where? I didn't hear anything,'.

'On the *phone*, Lucas. Not in the house. On the *phone*,'.

At this point I'm just standing there. Shaking.

'It's ok, Ivy. We'll go back to Holly and tell her, ok?' He takes
my hand and we walk into the sitting room.

'Lucas,' my voice is almost a whisper.

'You ok?'.

'I forgot to hang up,'.

Lucas runs back to the phone. I follow him. He picks up the
phone.

'Hello?' He says into the phone. 'You said something to me
before, say something else,' Lucas is shouting. He's scaring
me.

Scream

'Lucas, just hang up,' I tell him.

He doesn't hang up. He continues to shout into the phone at whoever is on the other end.

Lucas looks frightened.

'Ivy,' he says, trying to stay calm. 'Leave. Find Holly and Alice. Then leave!' He's panicking now.

'First, tell me what's happening,'.

'Ivy, just find Holly and Alice and *leave,*'.

'Ok,'.

I run and try to find Alice.

'Ivy?' Holly taps me on the shoulder. I jump. 'Are you ok? You look scared,'.

'Yeah... Lucas asked me to find you and Alice. We're leaving,'.

'No, we're not,'. she says.

'Yes, we are. Lucas and I will explain in the car. Come on, let's find Alice,'.

Holly and I run up the stairs.

'I'll go into the master bedroom. You check the smaller one. I'll meet you back here in a minute'. Holly tells me.

'Are you sure she's up here?'.

'Yes, Ivy. I'm 99% sure she is, I saw her come up a few minutes ago,'.

'Ok,' I walk into the small bedroom.

Nobody's in here. I walk out of the bedroom and go back to where Holly told me to meet her.

Alice walks out of the bathroom.

'Ivy!' She comes over to me.

'We're leaving,' I tell her.

'Wait, What? Why?'

'Lucas and I will explain to you and Holly in the car. We need to wait for Holly to come out of the master bedroom,'.

Alice and I stand at the top of the stairs waiting for Holly.

'Oh, you found her,' Holly says.

'I didn't find her, she found me,' I say.

We walk down the stairs to Lucas.

'You ready?' he asks.

'Yeah, let's go,'.

We walk back out to the car. Alice gets into the driver's seat. She starts the car and begins driving.

'Ok, are you going to tell us why we had to leave yet?' Holly asks

'Yes,' I reply. 'The house phone had started to ring, so Lucas picked up.

Lucas, you tell them what you heard,'.

'The person on the other end said: *Let me speak to Ivy or Holly.* I assumed it was one of your parents, but I don't think it was anymore. Ivy you tell them what happened next,'.

I take over. 'I kept saying *Hello?* And *Is anyone there?* But nobody said anything. I started thinking Lucas was playing some kind of joke on me, but then I heard a gunshot,' I tell them.

'Nice joke Ivy. Why did we have to leave?' Holly doesn't seem very convinced. Alice is concentrating on the road. She's gone pale.

'Holly... she's not joking,' Lucas says. 'Keep going Ivy,'.

I continue. 'I dropped the phone and told Lucas what I had heard. He thought I meant inside the house. But I told him it was on the phone. I was trying to stay calm, but I started overthinking it. I was terrified. I was standing there, in the hall with Lucas. Shaking. It was the scariest phone call I've ever had. Lucas and I then went into the sitting room to try and find Holly, but I forgot to hang up. The phone was still on the floor. We went back out to the hall. Lucas picked up the phone and put it to ear.

Hello? He said.

You said something to me before, say something else. He was shouting.

Then someone screamed. I told him to put the phone down but he wasn't listening. He was just shouting into the phone saying things like:

JUST SAY SOMETHING IT'S NOT THAT HARD.

YOU WERE TALKING A FEW MINUTES AGO!

WHAT KIND OF JOKE IS THIS?

JUST PLEASE SAY SOMETHING.

Then he hung up and told me to get you,'.

'Oh my *God*,' Holly says, smacking a hand over her mouth.

44

'That must have been *terrifying*,' Alice looks like she's just seen a ghost.

Lucas is silent for the rest of the car ride.

•••

Alice and I walk inside. We're quiet because out parents could be sleeping. We walk up the stairs. Neither of us say anything. I go to my room. Alice goes to hers.

I lock my door and put my pyjamas on. I pick up my favourite book and sit on my bed. I sit and stare at the wall, thinking about what happened tonight. *That was the most terrifying thing that has ever happened to me.*

I remember I have a book beside me, but I don't pick it up. That's not like me. I usually read when I'm scared, or stressed. But this time... I'm to scared to read. I'm to scared to do anything. I'm absolutely *terrified*. What if something else happens? What if someone is coming atter Holly and I.

I hear a knock on my door. I get up and unlock it.

'Hey Ivy... you ok?' Alice is at my door.

'Yeah. Just a bit scared still,' I say.

We walk over to my bed, and I sit down.

'You're not reading, Why's that?' she asks.

'I'm too scared Alice. I'm too scared something else is going to happen. I'm scared that someone is out to get Holly and I,' I tell her.

'Ivy, listen to me. If anything else happens, tell me straight away. Ok?' Alice walks over and sits with me, on my bed.

'Ok,' I reply. 'I'm going to sleep now,' I'm not actually, I uust want her to leave. I want to be by myself.

'Alright,' Alice gets up and walks to the door. 'Night, Ivy,' she leaves.

I get up from my bed and lock the door.

Five

Ivy

I'm lying in my bed staring at the ceiling. It's six a.m. It's bright out. I should get up. But I don't want to. I'm probably overthinking what happened last night. Nothing else is going to happen. It was probably just someone playing some kind of joke.

I get out of my bed and walk over to pull the curtains. I was expecting someone to have written on my window in blood, saying: *I'm watching you.* Or something like that. I'm just thinking about it too much.

I walk away from my window, and over to my wardrobe. I choose an outfit for today, and get changed. I'm wearing light blue jeans, and a sage green t-shirt.

Someone knocks on my door.

'Come in,' I say.

'I can't, the door is locked,' I hear my mums voice.

'Oh yeah, sorry,' I go to the door and unlock it. My mother walks in.

'What are you doing today, Ivy?' she asks.

'Uhm... I don't know yet. I'll text Holly and Lucas. Maybe we'll go to town,' I tell her, walking over to my mirror.

I start putting on a little bit of makeup, as I always do. Concealer, blush, and mascara.

'Alright, do you think you'll be leaving soon? You need breakfast,'.

'Yeah, I'll text them in a minute,'.

'Ok, let me know if you do go somewhere,'.

'I will, bye,' she turns around to leave.

'Bye,' my mum leaves my room. I go to the door to close, and lock it.

I sit on my bed and pick up my phone.

Me: Hey do you want to go to town?

Lucas: Ok when?

Me: Now maybe? Is that good for everyone?

Holly: That's fine.

Lucas: Ok!

Me: Where will we meet up?

Holly: The café?

Lucas: Yeah ok, that ok w/ you Ivy?

Me: Ok! I'll be there in abt five minutes.

Lucas: Alright, I'll be there in five minutes too.

Holly: I'll be a little late. My dad's annoying me about dresses to wear to his wedding. 10 mins promise.

Me: Ok.

Lucas: Cya in a few.

•••

I get up and put my phone in my pocket. I go over to my desk, and put on my fluorite, and carnelian bracelets. I also put on a clear quartz, crescent moon necklace.

I walk to my window ledge and pick out a couple of crystals to take with me. I choose rose quartz, amethyst, and my favourite, rhodonite. I take a rose incense stick, and a lighter. I light the
incense. Rose and strawberry are my favourite scents.

I grab my balck high top Converse, and put them on. I grab my tote bag, and look for the book I'm reading. I can't find it.

I just realised I fell asleep with it. Maybe it's under my blanket. I go to my bed, and lift the blanket. There it is.

I put my book in my bag and grab my crystals. I put the crystals in a little drawstring bag, and drop it into my tote. I take my headphones from my desk, and put them around my neck. I put out my incense.

I unlock my door and leave my room, closing it behind me. I walk down the stairs. I walk into the kitchen, where my mum, my dad, and Alice.

'I'm going now,' I tell them.

'Going where?' my dad asks.

'To town, with Holly and Lucas,'.

'Who's Lucas? Your boyfriend?'.

'*No* dad. Remember the boy with black hair? The one who was with Holly and I outside of the school?'.

'Oh yes. Now I remember. Have fun,' he says.

'Bye,'.

'Bye, Ivy,' my mum says. Alice gives me a wave and a look that says *be careful.*

I leave the house and start walking towards the café. My phone starts beeping, so I take it out of my pocket

Incoming Call

   Lucas

I answer the phone.

'Hi Lucas,' I say.

'Hi. I'm outside of the café,' he tells me.

'Ok, I'll be there in a second,' Lucas hangs up.

I finally get to the café, Lucas is standing outside.

'Hey,' he says.

'Hi. Should we wait outside for Holly? Or should we go in and tell

her we're inside?'. I ask.

'We can wait,' he tells me.

'Ok,'.

We stand outside of the café and wait for Holly to arrive.

Lucas looks at a black jeep. 'I think her dad drove her,'.

'Yeah, I think he did too,' I say.

Holly gets out of the car. She's wearing a light pink dress, and white Nike shoes.

'Hi!' she smiles.

'Hello,' Lucas says. I wave.

We walk into the cafe and sit down at a table.

'You want to know why I *really* took longer?' Holly asks.

'Why?' Lucas replies. I shoot Lucas a look that says *What did you get us into.*

'I wanted to see if Lucas would confess his love for Ivy,' she says in a sing-song voice.

'Shut up, Holly,' I say. Lucas is just sitting there.

•••

Holly, Lucas and I are walking down the street.

'Where are we going?' Holly asks.

'The bookshop. Ivy wants to go,' Lucas says.

'I never said that!' I laugh.

'I know, but you want to though. Don't you?'.

'Yes,' I say.

'Well, then. I know you *too* well,' he smiles. I smile back.

We walk into the bookshop. Holly runs off to the fantasy section.

'Holly's being really annoying,' Lucas says.

'I agree,'. We walk around the bookshop together, until we reach the *teen and YA* section.

'Choose a book. Or two if you want. I'll pay for them,' Lucas says.

'No, it's ok. You don't need to buy me anything,' I tell him.

'I know, but I want to,' He picks up a book and hands it to me. 'I think you'd like this,' he tells me.

'Thank you,' I say, taking the book. 'But i'm paying,'.

'No, you're not,' he takes the book from me and picks up another one from the shelf.

Holly walks over to us.

'Holly?' Lucas asks. 'Would you buy this book?' he shows her the book.

'Ok,' she says, picking up a copy.

Lucas walks to the counter, with the two books. He told me to wait here.

He comes back, holding a paper bag.

'We're going to read these, annotate them, and then give them to each other.' Lucas says.

'I don't want to annotate mine. It ruins the book,' Holly says.

'Ok, then. Lucas and I will do it then,' I say.

'Girls, both of you, at my house tonight. We're having a sleepover,' Lucas says.

'Ok!' I say.

'Sounds fun,' Holly adds.

Holly goes to the counter to pay.

'Holly!' Lucas calls.

'What?' she replies.

'I'm paying,'.

'Not for me, but you can buy your girlfriends,' Holly says.

'She's not my *girlfriend* Holly!'.

'Not *yet*,'. Holly pays for her book and Lucas pays for mine and his.

'Where are we going next?' Lucas asks.

'The art shop,' I tell them.

'Ok!' Holly says.

'I need new paint brushes,' Lucas says. Lucas paints. He's hoping to sell some pieces he's made.

We start walking towards the art shop.

Holly taps Lucas on the shoulder. 'When are you going to ask Ivy to be your girlfriend?'

'I don't know. Probably never,' Lucas replies. 'But for now, Holly. Please stop annoying me,'.

We walk into the art shop. Holly goes to look at sticky gem things. Lucas goes to look at paintbrushes.

'You bought me a book, so I'll buy you paintbrushes,' I tell Lucas.

'No, Ivy. Don't it's fine,'.

'That's what I said to you, but you didn't listen. So now, I won't listen,'

'Ivy, seriously—'

'No, Lucas. I'm buying you something,' I interrupt.

Lucas continues to look for paintbrushes. He picks up a set of them.

'These don't look too bad,' he says to himself. 'We're going to look at the paints now,' he grabs my hand and we walk to the paints.

Holly runs after us, with an uncountable amount of sticky gems.

'Are you sure you two aren't-'

'Be quiet!' I tell her. She's really starting to annoy me now.

We reach the paint aisle. Lucas is looking at the paints.

'Ivy?' Holly whispers in my ear.

'What?' I reply.

'Can you please answer one question?' she asks.

'Fine, only one,' I give in. She pulls me over to the aisle next to the paints.

'Do you like Lucas? Even the tiniest bit?' She's staring at me. She's literally not blinking.

'A tiny bit, not really though,' I tell her.

'LUCAS!' Holly shouts, running in his direction. 'IVY SAID SHE LIKES YOU THE TINIEST BIT!' she continues. *Oh my God.*

I walk back to the paint aisle, slightly embarrassed. Lucas looks at me, and Holly is jumping up and down. She's acting like an excited nine-year-old.

'I heard you Holly,' I tell her. I think she already knows that.

'I know. You were meant to hear me,'.

We walk over to the counter. Lucas puts his things up.

'I already said I'll pay, and I *don't* break promises,' I stand next to Lucas.

'And I said you're not paying,' he gives the lady behind the counter his money.

'Lucas, I'll give the money back to you,'.

'No you won't, Ivy. I won't let you,' the lady puts his things in a bag and gives it to him.

Holly puts her sticky gems on the counter next.

'How many are there?' Lucas asks.

'I don't know,' she replies.

'What will you use them for?' I ask.

'I'm not sure yet,'.

We walk out of the art shop.

'What next?' I ask

'Anywhere that sells sparkly silver dresses!' Holly says. 'I'm obsessed,'.

'Ok,' I say.

Lucas doesn't seem embarrassed by Holly annoying us. He seems to kind of *enjoy it*.

We finally reach a clothes shop that hopefully sells *silver sparkly dresses*. We walk inside. It's very hot here. Holly runs off again.

Lucas and I walk around, trying to find a fan. Once we finally spot one we sit down by it.

'I hate this shop. It's always really hot, and they have anything I'd wear,' I tell Lucas.

'Do you want to go somewhere that sells clothes that you *would* wear?'

'No, I have enough at home,'.

'You sure? We could go and have a look when Holly's done,'.

'I'm sure Lucas,',

'Ok,',

Holly comes running back with about ten colourful sparkly dresses, two of which are silver.

'I'm going to pay. You wait here,' she runs off again, not giving me or Lucas a chance to speak.

Holly comes back to us with a bag full of dresses.

'How many did you buy? Ten?' I ask.

'Fourteen,' she tells me.

We walk out of the shop. The cold air feels nice, it was so hot inside.

'Can we get drinks?' asks Lucas.

'Yeah, let's go,' I reply.

'Where will we get them?' Holly asks.

'The pound shop,' I say.

We enter the pound shop, and walk towards the drinks.

'What are you getting Ivy?' Holly asks.

'7 Up,' I tell her, picking up a can.

Lucas gets the same as me, and Holly gets Coke. We walk to the counter.

'It's my turn to buy something,' Holly takes the cans from Lucas and I.

We exit the pound shop and walk around, looking for somewhere to sit. We eventually sit down at a bench, in a local park.

'I'm going to go home soon and pack a bag for tonight,' I say.

'Yeah, same' Holly says.

•••

I walk into my house.

'Ivy? Is that you?' my mum calls, from the sitting room.

'Yeah,' I say walking into the sitting room. 'Can I have a sleepover tonight? Lucas invited Holly and I to stay at his place tonight,'.

'Ok, when will you be leaving?' she asks.

'I don't know, I'll ask in a while,' I tell her.

'Alright, Ivy. Go and pack your stuff then,'.

'Ok, thanks for letting me go,' I leave the sitting room and go upstairs.

'Hey,' Alice calls from her room.

'Hi,' I call back. I unlock my door and walk in.

I look around my room for a bag I could take with me, but I can't find anything.

'Alice!' I shout, walking out of my room.

'Yeah?' she shouts back.

I walk to her door and open it.

'Can I borrow a bag please? I'm going to a sleepover. Lucas asked Holly and I to stay over,'.

'Yeah, come in. I'll get you one now,' she gets up from her bed and walks to her wardrobe.

'Here,' she says, handing my a black bag. 'Is this ok?'.

'Yeah, it's perfect. Thanks,' I say walking to her door.

'Have fun,' she smiles.

Six

Holly

I step up to the front door. *Wow*. Lucas has a huge house. I
knock on it.

A man in a black suit answers the door.

'You must be Holly, come in,' he says. 'I'm Mr. Wright's butler, it's lovely to meet you,'. I had no idea Lucas was *this* rich.

'Hello, I'm Holly Jones. It's lovely to meet you too,' I smile. 'Lucas and your other friend, Ivy, are upstairs. I'll take you to the room,' he turns and walks up the stairs, I follow him.

'They're just in there,' the man tells me, pointing to a door. 'Thank you,' I say.

I open the door, Ivy and Lucas are laughing and smiling with each other. I really hope they do end up dating. I love them together.

'Hi!' Ivy jumps up from the carpet. She hugs me. Ivy doesn't hug me very often, unless she's excited about something.

'What are you so excited about, Ivy?' I ask. She says nothing.

Lucas also looks excited. Ivy Stops hugging me and sits back beside Lucas.

'What's going on?' I ask. 'Are you two dating or something?'. 'Yes,' Ivy smiles.

'FINALLY!' I run over and sit down with them. 'When did it happen?'.

'A few minutes before you got here,' Lucas tells me.

It's about time those two got together.

'I've been waiting *years* for this!' I say.

Lucas gives Ivy the book he bought her earlier.

'Thank you, Lucas,' she says.

I take mine out from my bag.

'Ok, Ivy and I will annotate ours. Holly, you just do whatever you like with yours.

'Ok,' I say.

Ivy

We all open our books. Holly starts reading straight away, but Lucas and I make little guides in the front of ours for the meanings of different colour tabs and highlighters.

Once we're done, we flip to the start of the book. We both start reading. Holly is a little bit ahead of us, but that's because she didn't have to sort out tabs and highlighter colours.

Holly's probably going to finish her book before Lucas and I finish ours. That's because we're writing and drawing in ours. Holly's not.

•••

We're all finished with our books now. It took Holly the longest to read it. She kept getting distracted.

We all started about 6:30 p.m. and it's now 10:45.

'Will we give the books to each other now?' Lucas asks.

'Ok,' I say.

He gives me the book he annotated, and I give him the one I did.

Lucas flips through the book.

'Your handwriting is amazing! And the little drawings are really cool,' he smiles.

'Thank you!' I decide to flip through mine.

His writing is nice too. He drew pictures on the pages too.

'Lucas— the drawings! *Wow*. How do you draw like this?'.

'Thanks, Ivy. I guess it's just a talent.

Someone knocks on the door.

'Come in,' Lucas says. The door opens and a man walks in.

'Hi, Lucas. Hi girls, I'm his dad. I came up just to make sure you're ok,'.

'Yeah, we're fine,' Lucas replies.

'Are one of the girls your girlfriend?' he asks. I wonder if Lucas will tell him the truth.

'Yes, Ivy is,'. I didn't expect him to actually tell him.

'Who's Ivy?'.

'The girl with brown hair is Ivy and the blonde is Holly,' Lucas tells him.

'Ok. Hi,' he says again.

'Hi, it's nice to meet you,' I smile.

'Hello," Holly gives an obviously forced smile.

'I'll leave you alone now, goodbye,' he leaves, not giving any of us a chance to say goodbye back.

'What should we do next?' Lucas asks.

'Should we dial our phone numbers?' Holly suggests.

'What do you mean?' I ask.

'Ivy, on your phone, dial your own number,' Holly tells me.

'Ok,' I pull out my phone and dial my number.

Lucas grabs my phone and presses the call button. It says there's an ongoing call. Lucas puts it on speaker mode.

'Hello?' the person on the other end says.

'Who are you?' I ask.

'I'm Ivy,' they say.

'How?' Lucas asks.

'I'm Ivy Greene,' they say.

'But... *I'm* Ivy Greene,' I tell them.

Holly jumps up, runs to the wardrobe and gets in to hide.

'Open your curtains, Lucas. I'm in your window,' they tell Lucas.

Lucas gets up. He doesn't seem to be afraid. He pulls the curtains open, and opens his blinds.

'I told you I'm here,' something says. I get up and walk to the window.

There's some weird drawing of a girl, in red paint or blood on the window.

'Whose number did you dial, Ivy?' Lucas asks.

'I dialled my own number. Look at my number on your phone and compare it to the one I dialled,' I tell him.

Lucas takes his phone out of his pocket and looks for my number.

'This is it right?' He shows me his screen, displaying my phone number.

'Yeah, it is. Look at the one I dialled,'.

He picks up my phone and looks at the number I dialled.

'They're the exact same...' he says.

'What's happening?' Holly's voice comes from the wardrobe.

'There's a drawing of a girl, in red paint, on the window!' I reply.

Holly pushes the wardrobe door open and steps out.

'Ivy, are you sure it's paint?' Lucas asks.

'I think it is. What else would it be?'

'Blood?' He suggests.

'Maybe,' I reply.

'I don't know... but I think we should just turn off our phones and close the curtains. That way, nobody can see or hear us,' Lucas says.

'Unless they're in the house,' I add.

'Turn on music, then they can't hear us,' Lucas tells me.

'Ok,' I go to his radio and turn it on. Music starts playing, but it's not loud enough, so I turn it up. 'Now if anyone *is* trying to hear us, they can't,'.

'We should just watch a movie and try to forget about all of this

weird stuff happening,' Holly suggests.

'Holly, I don't think we're *ever* going to forget this,' I tell her.

'But a movie doesn't sound too bad,'.

'Yeah alright, I'll put one on. Ivy, will you turn the music off please?' Lucas asks.

'Ok,' I get up and turn the music off.

'What will we watch?' Lucas asks.

'I don't know, let's just have a look and see if there's anything good,' Holly asks.

Lucas turns on the tv, and starts scrolling through movies we could watch.

Suddenly, the tv starts flickering on and off.

'What's happening, Lucas? Does this always happen?' I ask.

'No, this never happens,' he replies.

The tv stops turning on and off. A scene from some horror movie I've never heard of starts playing.

Wait... it's not a horror movie. It's not a movie at all. It's clips from the party we were at the other night. That looks like Lucas and I, when I was on the phone.

It suddenly flicks to a dimly lit room. A girl wearing a long, black, hooded, gown. I can't see her face, she's wearing a white mask.

Lucas and Holly are silent. I stay silent too.

Gunshot

'What...?' Lucas says, slowly.

'This is terrifying,' I add. Lucas picks up the remote and strats pressing the *off* button, violently.

'It's not going off!' He's panicking.

'Show me,' I grab the remote. '*God*. This stupid prankn is going too far now,'.

'We should go to the police,' Holly says.

'*No!*' I snap.

'Why not? Someone is like... *stalking* us, Ivy,' she argues.

'What are we going to say? *Someone is controlling our friend's tv and when I called my own number on my phone as a joke someone picked up saying it was me?*' I tell her.

'Exactly that, Ivy,' she says.

'They wouldn't believe us,' I tell her. 'They'd think we're some stupid teenagers playing with them. Plus, what can they even do?' .

After a few minutes, the video stops and the tv starts flickering on and off again.

'I don't like this,' Holly says.

'None of us do,' Lucas tells her.

'It's terrifying,' I add.

The tv finally stops flickering after about a half hour.

'That was weird,' I say.

'Only weird?' Holly snaps her fingers in my face a few times.

'We should probably sleep now,' Lucas finally says something. He's been silent ever since the tv stopped going on and off.

'Yeah I agree,' I reply.

'But it's only like twelve!' Holly slaps her hands down on the ground.

'I'm going to sleep. I'm done with tonight,' I stand up.

'Ok,' she says. 'If both of you are going to sleep I will too,' she continues.

'Where will we sleep?' I ask Lucas.

'There's a bed you can pull out under my bed. See the drawer?'

'Oh yeah, thanks,' I say.

I pull out the bed. I get Alice's bag, with my clothes and go into his bathroom to change.

Once I change I leave the bathroom and climb into bed.

•••

Lucas and I are waiting, quietly for Holly to wake up. She always sleeps in.

'How much longer do you think she'll be asleep for?' Lucas asks.

'Maybe another twenty minutes,' I reply.

She wakes up about forty minutes after.

'Hi!' Holly says.

'Morning,' Lucas gets out of bed.

'Will we interview Willow's parents today?' I ask Holly.

'Ok, I don't mind,' she also gets up. I decide I should get up too.

I take Alice's bag back into the bathroom and change. I'm not sure if we'll find out too much from Willow's parents. But it's worth a try.

I walk out of the bathroom. I'm wearing a light green hoodie and a black skirt. Holly is wearing one of her new sparkly dresses, this one is gold. Lucas is wearing a t-shirt and a tracksuit.

Seven

Ivy

Holly and I walk to the Evans' front door. Holly knocks.

'Hello?' the woman who answers the door says.

'Hi,' I say. 'I'm Ivy Greene, and this is my friend, Holly Jones.
Are you Mrs. Evans?'

'Yes, I am,' she tells me.

'We were wondering if we could interview you and Mr. Evans?' I ask.

'Is this about Willow?'.

'Yes, it is. Would you mind if we asked a few simple questions about her? Holly and I are trying to solve her case,'.

'Yes, of course. I'll take any opportunity to find out what happened to Willow. Come in,' we walk in. Mrs. Evans shows us to her living room.

We all sit down.

'Alright, girls. Start whenever you like,' Mrs. Evans tells us.

'I'll start in just a minute, but for now I was wondering if Mr. Evans is here too?' I ask.

'Yes, I'll get him now,' she stands up and goes upstairs.

About two minutes later, she comes back, Mr. Evans is following her. They both sit down.

'So you'd like to ask some questions about Willow?' Mr. Evans asks.

'Yes, if you don't mind,' I say.

'Ok, start whenever you're ready,' he tells Holly and I.

'Is it ok if I record the interview,' I ask.

'Of course, do whatever you need,' he says.

•••

I sit down at my desk and open my laptop. I begin to type down the transcript.

•••

Transcript

Ivy: Did you know Willow's friends?

Mrs Evans: Willow didn't have very many
friends. I know a lot of people are glad
she's gone.

Ivy: Do you have any idea why people are
glad she's gone?

Mrs Evans: I don't know. I don't know what
she did. She didn't talk to me or her father
very much.

Ivy: So you don't think many people liked
Willow?

Mrs Evans: No, I don't think Willow was
liked by many people.

Ivy: Do either of you know if Willow was fighting with someone before her disappearance?

Mr Evans: I don't think she was fighting with anyone, but she *has* threatened to run away before.

Holly: Do you think she was serious?

Mr Evans: I don't know. Willow was usually serious about things, but I don't know if she did run away. I think something happened. I don't think she'd leave for four years. If she did run away, it would probably only have been for a couple of days. Willow would get bored on her own.

Holly: What was the last thing Willow said to you both before she disappeared?

Mr Evans: Both of us were in the kitchen when Willow came in and told us she was going to the forest. She said to us *"I'm going to the woods. Goodbye, I'll be back soon,"*.

Ivy: Thank you, that's all we need for now.

• • •

Once I'm finished typing out the transcript, I walk to my bed and flip through my book that Lucas annotated for me.

Holly

I walk across the hall into my brother, Noah's room.

'Would you knock next time?' he snaps.

'Sorry. I'm bored, I need something to do,' I tell him.

'Well, that's not my problem,' Noah is a year older than Ivy, Lucas and I, he's sixteen and we're fifteen.

'Sorry,' I leave his room and close the door behind me.

I start walking down the stairs, when I notice Lucas at the bottom.

'Hi!' I call, I start running down the steps.

'Be careful, Holly. You're going to fall,' he tells me. I get to the bottom of the stairs.

'Why are you here?' I ask. 'That sounded rude, sorry,'.

'Noah asked me to come over to play some new game he got,'.

'Oh, ok. I'm going to Ivy's, you should come when you're done with Noah,' I suggest.

'Ok, see you later,' he walks up the stairs.

Ivy never asked me to go to her house, But I usually just show up without telling her. She doesn't mind.

I leave my house and start walking to Ivy's. Her house isn't too far from mine. We live in the same estate. It's about a two minute walk.

I get to Ivy's door. I just walk in. That's what I always do and that's what she does when she comes to my house too.

I run up the stairs.

'Hi, Holly,' Alice says.

'Hi!' I reply, knocking on Ivy's door.

Ivy opens her door.

'Hi,' she says.

'Hi,' I walk into her room.

We both sit on her bed.

'What were you doing before I came?' I ask her, trying to start a conversation.

'Reading,' she replies.

'What book?'.

'The one Lucas gave me,'.

'You already read that,' I tell her.

'I know, I just want to see what he wrote,'.

We're silent for a few minutes. It's not awkward though. Ivy and I can do anything together and it wouldn't be weird.

'Who do you like, Holly? I'm going to annoy you about it, just like you annoyed Lucas and I,'.

'You'll laugh at me,' I still haven't told her the truth about myself.

'I won't laugh at you,' she tells me.

'Well, if you don't laugh, you'll *hate* me,'.

'I won't hate you,'.

'Well—'.

'No more excuses. Who do you like?' I don't want to tell her.

'What's happening?' Alice asks, opening Ivy's bedroom door.

'Nothing,' I say. I can't tell them. Not yet.

'Holly won't tell me who she likes,' Ivy tells Alice. 'At least give me a hint!' she pleads.

'It's probably not who you expected it to be,' I tell her

'Could you tell us the gender?' Alice asks.

'No,' I tell her.

'Is it a girl?' Alice asks. 'I won't judge, I promise,'.

'No,'.

'I have a boyfriend,' Ivy tells us. I think it was more directed to Alice.

'Who?' Alice looks excited.

'Lucas,' she tells her.

'Since when?' Alice asks.

'Yesterday,' Ivy responds.

'I like a girl,' Alice tells us.

'I already know who!' Ivy tells me.

'I'm pansexual. A lot of people don't know what that is,' Alice tells me.

'What is it?' I ask.

'It's when a person likes everyone. It doesn't matter their gender or gender identity,' Alice explains.

'Oh,' I say.

'Who do you like, Hol?' Ivy asks again.

'It's someone we know,' I tell them.

Ivy hugs me.

'I told you I wouldn't hate you!' she says.

'That's because you don't know who,'.

'I still won't hate you. I could never hate you,' she tells me.

Alice is sitting on Ivy's bed, smiling.

'Let's go to the back garden,' Alice suggests.

'Ok,' Ivy says, letting go of me.

We go downstairs, through the kitchen and into the garden. We sit on a bench.

The three of us spend the evening talking. It's nice, being Able to talk to Ivy's sister like this. She's older than us and I know Ivy can trust her not to tell anyone anything we tell her.

•••

I get home and change for bed. Once I'm changed I go straight to bed. It's only nine p.m. but I'm tired. I slept in late this morning, but I'm still tired. I lie in bed staring at the ceiling. I wasn't expecting to come out to Ivy today. I *especially* wasn't expecting to come out.

Ivy and Alice know part of the secret I've been keeping for about a year now. They still don't know that I like Alice.

I grab my phone from my nightstand. There's a message.

?: Willow Evans isn't the only one who will disappear.

I'm shaking. I sit up and read it again.

Willow Evans isn't the only one who will disappear.

I put my phone down, but it starts vibrating, so I check it.

?: Open your front door. A girl wants sweets.

I don't know what's happening. I don't want to answer the door.

Knock

I stand up and leave my room. I run downstairs and try to find a packet of sweets for the little girl '?' said would be at my door. I think to myself: *The scariest part of this is, Lucas and Noah are gone. My dad is at work.*

I find a little bar of chocolate. I run to the door and open it. 'Hello, Holly,' a girl wearing a long dress and a mask is standing at my front door. Her hair is messy. It's long and black. Her dress is also black. Her mask covers her whole face.

I hand her the chocolate bar without saying a word. 'Goodbye, I'll be back soon,' she says.

The girl turns around and walks away.

I close my door and run back upstairs and into my room. I lock my door and sit on my bed.

Goodbye, I'll be back soon.

That's the last thing Willow said to her parents before she disappeared.

I pick up my phone to see if I've gotten any more texts. But there's nothing else.

I text Ivy and tell her about the text. I don't mention the girl at my door though.

I lie in my bed again. This time I fall asleep. I'm sleeping for about an hour when I get woken up by Noah. He's panicking over something.

'What's wrong Noah?' I ask.

'Someone is in the house,'.

Eight

Ivy

   Holly left about two hours ago now. She texted me and said she got a text from someone called '?'. It was that Willow isn't the only one who will go missing.
'Ivy!' Alice calls. 'Ivy, there was a letter in the door, I have it here,' she hands me a letter. 'It doesn't say who it's from,'.

I look at the letter. It says

To: Ivy Greene
Address: **********
From: ?

It's from '?'.

'Alice...' I say. 'This is from the same person who texted Holly,'.

'What?'.

'Remember, I told you that Holly got a text saying *Willow isn't the only one who will disappear,'* I remind her.

'Oh, yeah. That must be the person who was asking for you or Holly at the party. And whoever answered when you called your phone. It's probably the same person who drew on Lucas' window and controlled his tv too,' Alice says.

'It *is* them. *Question mark* is probably behind Willow's disappearance,' I tell Alice.

Alice leaves my room so I can open the letter alone. She told me it might be private and I might not want her to know what it said.

I tear open the letter. I unfold it and read what it says. I'm terrified to start reading, but I start anyways.

Ivy Greene.

I know everything I need to know about you. I could make you disappear, just like Willow did. I can do whatever I like with you. I know where you live, Ivy. I know where Holly lives. Though I only really care about you and Holly, I have Lucas' address too. I'm going to make someone disappear. I've already told Holly this and I think she's told you. But Ivy Greene, this is your warning. Make one wrong move trying to solve this case and I will end your life. Show anyone this letter, or tell anyone about it and I will end them too. Nobody other than you, Holly, Lucas and Alice know about me. I don't care about Lucas or Alice, but they just happen to be around when I make my moves. Ivy, someone close to you will go missing within the next two months. Be prepared for it. If you tell Holly, Alice, or your little boyfriend Lucas what I'm telling you right now, I'll make sure you regret it for the rest of your life. Ivy, I'm warning you. ONE MISTAKE AND YOU WILL DIE. Your life will be ended. Holly hasn't gotten a letter. You should feel special my darling. I'm writing you a letter. Holly got two short texts. Oh wait your friend hasn't told you about the second text, or who was at her door. That's right Miss Ivy Greene. I was at Holly's door. I told her a girl was at her door and she wanted sweets. She gave me a bar of chocolate. You don't know where I'm writing this. Do you? Oh you probably do. Little Miss Ivy knows absolutely everything. You think you know a lot about Willow. But do you really? Don't make any more assumptions that you know who Willow was. And I'm not going to tell you where I'm writing this letter. You'll have to figure that out yourself. But will you figure out who I am? No. You can't solve a murder for your life. Unless it's a fake one you bought online. You're making no progress with the case. You'll never solve it. Someone will tell you. But you won't solve it. You'll be told by someone who I know. I know that person very well, Ivy. Good luck trying to figure out who I am. You'll never find out. My dear, it's pointless what you're doing. You think you're helping solve this. The case is closed for a reason, darling. By the way I was the one who called at the party. I was the one who answered the phone on the sleepover. I drew on the window. I hacked the tv. Ivy, you have no idea what I am capable of. Do not underestimate my power. If anyone asks what this was, tell them it was just a drawing. A stupid drawing of something random. You make up what it is. Stick to the story, Ivy.

Expect to hear from me soon.

Love,

?

What did I just read? That was the scariest thing I've read. I'm being threatened. I *want* to tell someone, but I *can't*. I'm shaking so hard. I thought the phone call was scary. I thought the sleepover was scary. But this... this is absolutely *terrifying*.

I'm going to burn this letter. I stand up and walk to my window ledge, where I have a lighter, the letter is still in my hand. I fold the letter back up. I place it on a metal plate. I pick up my lighter.

The paper ignites. I watch it burn, slowly. The flame goes out. Charcoal smoke fills the room.

I pull open my window. The smoke takes a while to clear. I stand there, at my window. I stare at the ashes.

I picked up an incense stick and lit it to get rid of the smell. I don't want my parents to think I was burning things.

Someone knocks on my door.

'Ivy?' Alice's voice comes from the other side of the door.

'Can I come in?' she asks.

'Yeah, ok,' I tell her.

Alice opens the door. 'What was the letter?' she asks. I almost forget what I'm supposed to tell her.

'Just a drawing of... uhm... flowers. I don't know who it was from. It said it was someone I knew. I burned it. Just don't tell mum and dad I burned it. They'll kill me,' I say.

'Don't worry, I won't say anything. I'll leave you alone,'.

'Thanks Alice, bye,'.

Alice leaves my room and closes the door behind her.

This person don't need to tell me where they write that letter. I know. They're in Holly's house.

I pull out my phone and text Holly. I hope she's not home. I hope her and Noah are ok.

Me: Holly? Where are you?

Me: Holly!!!!!

Me: HOLLY!

Me: HOLLY PLEASE!!!

Me: HOLLY ARE YOU OK?

Me: HOLLY OH MY GOD PLEASE ARE YOU OK?? IS NOAH OK??

Holly's not answering. She's not answering and I'm panicking. *OH MY GOD!*

I grab my bag from the end of my bed. My phone is still in my hand.

I run to the door. I run down the stairs. I open the front door and leave. I leave without telling anyone where I'm going. I leave without letting anyone know I'm leaving.

I run down the street as fast as I can. I'm running past houses. I'm almost at her house.

I reach her front door. I'm suddenly banging on it as hard as I possibly can.

Nobody comes to the door. People are screaming inside.

I grab the handle of the door and push it down. I run inside without closing the door behind me.

'HOLLY!' I scream. 'NOAH? ARE YOU OK?' I run up the stairs.

'IVY!' I hear Holly's voice come from her bedroom.

'HOLLY I'M COMING!' I shout.

'IVY! HURRY!' She sounds terrified.

I get to her bedroom door. I open it and run in.

Holly is on her bedroom floor shaking.

'Holly!' I say. 'Are you ok? What happened?' I ask.

'Someone— someone is in the house,' she tells me.

'I know. But who?' I ask. *Oh God, that was a stupid question. I already have an idea who.*

'Ivy, how am I supposed to know that?' she snaps.

'Sorry. Stupid question. It's that 'question mark' person. Convince me it's not,'.

'HELP!' Noah's voice is coming from the bathroom.

'NOAH! HELP HIM!' Holly screams at me.

'COME WITH ME!' I tell her.

'I CAN'T!'.

'WHY?'.

'MY ARM!' she screams.

'WHAT DO YOU MEAN?' *another stupid question.*

'I WAS *SHOT!*' she screams again.

'WHAT! ARE YOU O—'.

'JUST GET NOAH!' she screams once more.

'ALRIGHT,'.

I run out of her room and into the bathroom.

Noah is on the bathroom floor. He doesn't look harmed. He's not shaking. He looks fine. He probably isn't fine, though. So I ask, 'Noah, are you ok?' I sit down on the bathroom floor beside him.

'Are you ok?' I ask.

'Yeah. Someone came into the bathroom. I got scared and screamed,' he tells me.

'Ok, as long as you're alright,'.

'Thanks for coming over. The person ran out of the bathroom, downstairs and left through the back door when I screamed for help,'.

'We're taking Holly to the hospital,' I say.

'What? Why? Is she ok?' he asks.

'She was shot. We need to get her to the hospital,' I tell Noah.

Noah and I stand up and run out of the bathroom.

'Holly!' Noah runs over to his sister, who is still on the floor and holds her in his arms. 'Holly, are you ok? Ivy told me what happened,'.

'I'm fine,' she tells him.

'We're going to take you to the hospital,' I sit down on the floor with Noah and Holly.

'I said I'm fine, Ivy. I don't need to go to the hospital,'.

'Holly, you're going to need stitches and you're losing a lot of blood right now,' I explain. 'Noah, pick her up and take her to your car,' I instruct.

Noah stands up. He bends down and takes Holly back into his arms again. I also stand up.

I run down the stairs as fast as I can without falling. If I could, I would throw myself down the stairs but I can't do that, so I don't.

I grab Noah's keys from a table in the hall. I run outside to his car and unlock it. I open one of the doors at the back of the car so Noah can put Holly in. I'm not even paying attention to what side of the car I'm on.

Noah runs out the front door.

'Ivy!' he calls. 'Ivy, I need my keys to lock the door!' He stands there at the front door like an idiot.

'Just get her in the car. While you're doing that, I'll lock it!' I call back.

Noah runs to the car. I run to the door. I shove the key into the keyhole and twist them around. I check to make sure that the door is locked before pulling the key back out.

I run back to the car. Noah is sitting in the front seat, waiting for his keys so he can start the car.

I go to the back seat. I sit beside Holly. I throw the keys to Noah. He starts the car. Suddenly, we're driving.

Noah is going as fast as he can on this road. We don't live too far from the hospital. It's about a five minute drive away.

My parents and Alice are probably spam texting me to make sure I'm alive.

I check my phone. I was right. My mum and dad have been calling and texting me. Alice was texting me.

I open my mum's texts first.

Mum: Ivy where are you?

Mum: Ivy text me please

Missed call

Missed call

Mum: Ivy please be safe

Mum: Ivy you're scaring me

Mum: Your dad is going to call you

Missed call

Missed call
Wow. She's worried.
I open my dad's texts.

Dad: Ivy r u alive?

Dad: Ivy yer mum said ur not texting her back

Dad: Ivy don't ignore ur mother

Missed call

Missed call

Missed call

Missed call

Missed call

My dad seems to think I'm *ignoring* them. I don't think he understood what mum told him.

I open Alice's texts.

Alice: Ivy where r u mum and dad are freaking out

Alice: Ivy please just let one of us know that ur ok

Alice: Ily <3

I might have scared my family, but I don't regret it one bit. My best friend could lose too much blood and *die*. The last thing I'm going to do is tell anyone where I'm going. I'm helping Holly. That's all I care about at the minute.

Maybe I should text one of them back.

Me: Alice tell mum and dad im alr but Holly's not I left bc I felt something was wrong over at her house. She was shot and she's losing a lot of blood. I'm in the back of Noah's car with her atm we're on the way to the hospital. She's gonna need it stitched. Sorry I didn't tell any1 where I was going. I was just worried abt Holly. I needed to run over to her house. I didn't know she was shot. I just had a feeling smth was wrong so I went over. Tell mum and dad if they need me I'll be at the hospital with Holly. Ily <3

Alice: OMG IS SHE OK?

Me: I THINK SHE'S FINE. SHE'S NOT TALKING VERY MUCH THOUGH.

Alice: Tell her I hope she's ok :)

Me: Ok! We're finding a parking spot now gtg cya <3

Alice: Bye ly <3

Me: Lyt :)

We find a parking spot. Noah opens his car door and climbs out. He runs around to the back of the car, opens Holly's door and lifts her out.

We run into the emergency room.

I sit down on a chair in the waiting area while Noah talks to a doctor.

A few minutes later, he walks over to me. Holly is no longer in his arms. Tears are streaming down his face.

'What's happening?' I ask. 'Where did they take Holly?'.

'They're taking her to emergency surgery to get the bullet removed,' he explains.

'Do they think she's going to be ok?'.

'They think she'll make it,' he tells me. He's crying hard. 'I just hope she's ok,' he sits down leaving a chair between us and starts sobbing.

I pull out my phone and text Lucas.

Me: Lucas get to the hospital rn

Lucas: Why?

Me: I'll explain when ur here. I'm in the emergency room.

Lucas: Ok be right there. Bye <3

Me: Bye <3

I put my phone back in my bag and turn to Noah. He's still crying.

'She's going to be ok. I know she will,' I tell him, reassuringly.

'I hope so...' his voice is weak and shaky.

After waiting for about twenty minutes, I see Lucas enter the waiting area.

He spots Noah and I and runs over to us.

'What happened?' he asks immediately.

'Holly was shot,' I tell him.

'What— when?' he sits in the empty chair between Noah and I.

'I'm not sure. I got a feeling something was happening over at Holly's house so I ran over. Someone had broken in while Holly and Noah were home. I ran upstairs and into Holly's room. She was on the floor. She told me that she was shot,' I say. I continue explaining everything that happened.

'You just... had a feeling?' Lucas asks, confused.

'Yeah, I guess,' I reply. I'm not great at lying, so I'm not sure if he's convinced or not.

'Oh,' Lucas says.

'We probably should have called an ambulance but we didn't think of that at the time,' I say.

We've been waiting for an hour in the waiting area now. No doctors or nurses know what is going on in the operating room. I hope Holly's ok.

Noah called his and Holly's parents to let them know what happened.

A nurse is walking past us.

'Excuse me?' I say, trying to get her attention.

'Yes?' she stops.

'I was wondering if you had any updates on Holly Jones?' I play with a ring on my finger.

'Yes, she should be out of surgery soon,' she tells me.

'Thank you,' I say.

I look over at Lucas and Noah. They're both sleeping. How did they fall asleep? The hospital is noisy.

I tap Lucas on the shoulder.

'Lucas,' I say. 'Lucas wake up!' I tap him again.

Lucas opens his eyes slowly.

'Hi,' he says quietly. 'Anything on Holly?'.

'Yes, but we have to wake Noah first,' I tell him.

'Ok,' Lucas turns away from me and faces Noah.

'Noah,' Lucas whispers, tapping Noah's head. 'Wake up!' He taps his head again.

Noah's eyes open.

'What? Did you say something?' he asks.

'Holly should be out of surgery soon,' Lucas tells him.

'Really?' Noah sits up in his seat.

'Yep,' I say.

Noah's eyes light up. He acts like he hates his sister, but everyone knows that he would do anything for her.

A doctor walks over to us. She looks a little like Jade Evans. 'You're Holly's friends right?' she asks.

'Yes,' I answer.

'Oh, Ivy. It's nice to see you again,' so she is Jade. Willow's cousin.

'I had no idea you were a doctor,' I say.

'Yeah, I'm a few years older than Willow. She'd probably be in college now if she was still here. Willow was in her last year of school when she disappeared. I was in my fourth year of medical school. I've been a doctor for two years now,' she explains.

'Oh, I thought you and Willow were the same age!' I reply. I didn't think that though. I just wanted to try and start a conversation because I'm so bored. I've been sitting here for hours now.

Jade pulls a pen out of her pocket and starts clicking it. I can't help but think: *God that's so irritating.*

'Any information on my sister?' Noah asks.

'Didn't Ivy just ask a doctor that a minute ago?' Lucas looks at Noah.

'Holly is in recovery. She should be fine within the next four weeks. Her arm is bandaged up and it will be in a sling for four weeks. She should be fine after that,' Jade tells us.

'So can we see her?' Noah asks.
'Yes. I'll show you to her room,'.

I wake up to see Ivy, Noah and Lucas sitting in my hospital room. Lucas is asleep and so is Ivy. Her head is resting on Lucas' shoulder. I love those two so much. They're the best friends I could ask for.

Noah looks over at me. He notices I'm awake. He jumps out of the chair he's sitting in and hurry's over to me.

'Holly!' he says. He runs back to Ivy and Lucas. He starts shaking Lucas, but he doesn't touch Ivy.

Lucas wakes up.

'Oh my God, Noah. You didn't have to *shake* me awake. I'm not a heavy sleeper,' he snaps.

'*Sorry*. Wake Ivy up,' Noah tells Lucas.

'Ok,' Lucas replies.

Lucas leans down to Ivy's ear and whisper's something I can't hear.

Ivy slowly opens her eyes.

'Hi,' she says quietly. 'Is Holly still asleep?' she closes her eyes again.

'She's awake,' Noah tells her.

Ivy opens her eyes again and gets up slowly.

'Holly!' she says, walking over to me. 'Are you ok?' she asks.

'I'm fine,' I tell her.

'Are you sure?'.

'I'm fine,' I repeat.

Ivy sits on the edge of the hospital bed.

Noah walks back over to me.

'Noah, can I talk to Holly for a minute, please?' Ivy asks.

'Yeah, ok,' Noah walks back to Lucas, who is still half asleep in a chair.

'What's wrong?' I ask.

'I think we should give up on the case,' she says.

'What? Why?'.

'Everything that is happening is because we're trying to solve the case. Someone doesn't want us to know what happened to Willow,'.

'If we give up that just means that someone will get what they want, Ivy,' I tell her.

'Holly. Think. Look where we are because of this. Wouldn't it be better to give up and be safe than to keep going and be in danger?'.

She has a point.

'I guess,'.

'We're done with the case,' Ivy tells me.

'Ok,' I say.

'Oh, by the way, do you remember Jade?' Ivy asks.

'Obviously. She's hard to forget,'.

'She's a doctor here,' she tells me.

'Oh,' I was *not* expecting to hear that.

'Jade was a few years older than Willow,' Ivy says. She continues telling me things about Willow that Jade has told her when she was talking to her.

'I thought they were the same age,' I say.

'I knew they were a few years apart but I pretended not to know because I was bored,' Ivy tells me.

'Wow, Ivy. Lying out of boredom? Are you ok?' I sit up.

Ivy usually don't lie unless it's for a good reason, so her lying just because she's bored is *really* weird

Lucas picks up his phone and calls his dad to pick us up from the hospital. We're still sitting in Holly's room.

'My dad said he'd get the driver to pick us up. Do you want to come back to my place?' Lucas asks.

'Yeah, ok. I'm just going to text my mum and tell her,'.

'Alright,' he smiles.

I take my phone out from my bag and begin texting my mother.

Me: I'm going to Lucas' house be home later :)

Mum: thats fine is holly ok

Me: Yeah she's fine now

Mum: ok see u later ivy

Me: Bye

  I put my phone back into my bag.

'Yeah mum said she's fine with me going,' I tell Lucas.

'Great,' he replies.

  Lucas and I have been sitting down in silence for the past ten minutes.

Lucas' phone beeps.

'The drivers outside,' He tells me.

'Alright,' I say. 'Bye Holly, bye Noah,' I smile at them. Lucas says the same as I did and we walk out.

  We reach the doors and Jade is standing there.

'Thank you, Jade. Holly and I won't be continuing to work on the case anymore. We have a good reason to stop. Thanks for everything,' I smile.

'Oh that's ok. I wasn't expecting you to continue with it for much longer. The police couldn't figure out what happened to her, after all. Thanks for trying,' She gives a small wave.

  Lucas and I walk out of the doors and try to find the car.

'There it is,' Lucas says, pointing at a fancy black jeep.

  We walk towards it and get in.

'I wasn't expecting this to happen,' Lucas says, as the driver turns his keys.

We pull up in Lucas' driveway. I put my hand on the door handle when Lucas stops me.

'He'll get the doors,' Lucas tells me, talking about the driver.

The driver opens Lucas' door first. He climbs out of the car. The driver walks over to me and opens my door. I get out. Lucas is waiting for me at the front door.

I walk to the front door and Lucas opens it. He gestures for me to enter the house first.

We both walk up the stairs.

'Ivy, come here,' Lucas tells me.

He puts his arm around me and we walk to a door. Lucas opens it. It's a dark room.

It can't be Lucas right? Lucas isn't that question mark person is he? Is he going to lock me in here?

Lucas turns on the light. It's an art studio. I can't believe I actually thought he would keep me here.

'Wow,' I say, walking around. There are paintings everywhere. 'The paintings are *amazing*!' I tell him.

'Thanks,' he smiles. 'I didn't think you'd like them,'.

'What! Of course I like them! They're great!'.

My eyes keep flickering to one painting of a beach with a sunset. It's the most basic but beautiful thing I've ever laid eyes on.

'That's my favourite,' I tell Lucas, pointing to it.

'It reminds me of you,' he tells me. 'I'm not sure why. I've never been to a beach with you,'.

I just smile.

We leave the art studio and go to his room. I sit on his bed.

'You ok?' Lucas asks.

'Yeah, I'm ok,' I say. 'It's so hot today,'. Summer is starting and it's getting warmer.

'I have a pool out the back. Will we get in?' Lucas asks.

'Uhm... I don't have anything to wear,' I say.

'I have something you can wear,'.

'Ok,'.

Lucas walks to his *huge* wardrobe and pulls out something. He walks back over to me and hands me a green bikini.

'You can change into this if you'd like,' Lucas tells me.

'Alright, I'll go to the bathroom. I won't be long,' I say.

'Ok,' he says.

I walk to his bathroom and enter. I change into the mint green bikini he gave me.

I can't stop thinking about him. His black hair. His green eyes. The way he smiles at me. The way he talks. He's perfect.

I look in the mirror. I hate this. I look stupid. This is why I don't wear these things.

I leave the bathroom. Lucas has changed too. I left my clothes in the bathroom.

'Is your dad here? I haven't noticed him,' I ask as we walk out of Lucas' bedroom.

'No he's working,' Lucas tells me.

'Oh,'.

We walk downstairs, through his living room and to his back door. The pool is right in front of the door. I swear I'm not lying when I say It's almost bigger than my back garden.

'Shit, I forgot towels. One minute,' Lucas makes his way out of the living room. I don't know where he goes next.

I sit down on the floor while I wait for him to come back.

'Hey,' I hear Lucas' voice. 'Sorry,' he walks back into the sitting room.

'It's ok, don't apologise,'.

We go outside. Lucas sets the towels down on a table by the pool.

I'm standing on the edge of the pool. Suddenly I'm not standing. I'm in the freezing water. Lucas pushed me in.

'OH MY GOD!' I shout at him. I start laughing as I climb back out. 'It's cold in there,' I tell him.

'Yeah?'.

'Yeah!'

I stand next to Lucas, who is now a little bit wet from the splash I made, falling into the pool.

Lucas looks away, so I take this as an opportunity to get him back for pushing me in.

I walk around a bit until I'm behind him. I put my hands on his back and push him into the blue tinted pool.

'GOD IT'S COLD!' he laughs.

'I told you that!' I say, sitting on the side of the pool.

Lucas makes his way towards me and lifts me up and throws me over his shoulder.

'What are you doing?' I ask.

'Making you get in with me,' he tells me, putting me down into the water.

The water is cold against my skin. Lucas' arms are still around my waist.

Lucas lets go of my waist and starts swimming towards a float.

He picks up the float and throws it to me. He swims back with another float.

I try to get onto the float when I notice something written on the float in black.

'Lucas?'.

'Yeah?'.

'What's that?' I ask.

'What's what?'.

I put my finger on the writing.

Not recommended for small children

I couldn't be more embarrassed.

'Nevermind,' I say, my face turning a light shade of pink.

I swim underwater to hide the shade my face was turning.

We both mess around and annoy each other in the pool for an hour or so.

'It's getting cold, I'm going to get out,' I say. I'm starting to shake because of how cold it is.

'Ok, I'll get out too,' Lucas tells me.

We both climb out of the pool. We walk towards the table where Lucas left the towels.

I grab one of them and wrap it around me. Lucas does the same.

He takes my hand and we walk back inside the house. We make our way up the stairs and into Lucas' room.

'I'll change in the bathroom again,' I tell Lucas, walking to the bathroom.

'Alright,' he smiles.

I walk into the bathroom. I change back into my clothes. The water is dripping from my hair. The bathroom floor is going to be *soaked*.

Once I'm changed I notice a spare towel on a towel rack. I pick up the towel and dry the floor.

Suddenly, I hear a knock on the bathroom door.

'You ok?' Lucas asks.

'Yeah, I'll just be a second. I'm just drying the floor,' I explain.

'What? Are you dressed?,'.

'Yeah, I'm dressed,'.

Lucas walks into the bathroom.

'What are you doing? Give me that. Don't worry about drying the floor, Ivy. It'll dry with the air,' Lucas says, taking the towel from my hand.

'Ok,' I say.

Lucas picks me up off of the floor and carries me to his bed. He sits me down on the side of the bed.

'Ivy, listen. The floor will dry by itself. It's hot inside,' Luas tells me, brushing my hair behind my ear with one hand, the other on my cheek.

'Ok,' I smile.

Lucas sits next to me.

'Should we get coffee?' he asks.

'Yeah, sure,'.

We stand up. I grab my bag and Lucas grabs his. We walk out of the room and go downstairs. We put on our shoes and leave the house. Lucas locks the door behind him.

We get into the car.

'Could you take us into town plese?' Lucas asks the driver.

The driver nods in response.

I think the driver might be paid extra for not talking.

We make it into town. Lucas thanks the driver as we climb out of the car.

We walk down the street to the coffee shop. We enter the small building and walk to the counter to order.

'What would you like, Iv?' Lucas asks.

'A caramel latte and a chocolate doughnut, please,'.

'Ok. Can we get two caramel lattes and two chocolate doughnut please?'.

'Yep. That will be ten pounds please,' the girl behind the counter says.

Lucas hands her the money.

'Thank you. It shouldn't take long,'.

Lucas and I stand to the side and wait while our order is being prepared.

Our order is called so we take our drinks and doughnuts.

We thank the girl and sit down at a table.

'So you and Holly aren't going to be working on the case anymore?'.

'No, I think it's too risky. I think the stalking is because we're trying to figure out what happened to Willow,' I explain.

'Oh,'.

'I think I might just go to the Willow's house and let her parents know that we've stopped doing this,'.

'Yeah, ok. We can go once we're finished with our doughnuts. We can take the coffee with us,' Lucas tells me.

'Aright. Thank you,'.

Once we're done we leave and go back to the car.

I give the driver directions to the house.

'Do you think they'll be disappointed?' Lucas asks.

'Yes. I do think they'll be disappointed. They have every reason to be disappointed. More people have given up on their daughter,'.

We arrive at the Evans' house. Lucas and I get out of the car and make our way to the door.

I ring the doorbell. It takes a while for somebody to open the door.

Mrs. Evans is standing at the door.

'Ivy! Hello. Come in,' she says, with a hopeful expression on her face.

'You go, Ivy I'll wait here,' Lucas tells me.

'Ok,' I say.

I enter the house. Mrs. Evans takes me to the living room again. Mr. Evans is already on the sofa.

'Ivy is here. Remember her?'.

'Yes, I do,' he says.

I sit down in the same spot I sat the last time I was here.

'Any news on Willow?' Mrs. Evans asks.

'Uhm, well... I'm sorry to have to tell you this but Holly and I will no longer be working on the case as we have experienced stalking ever since we've started the case. I know it's disappointing but it's for our own safety. We have been getting messages threatening us saying things like "If you and your little friend don't stop trying to solve this case you'll regret it" and other things similar to that. Again I am so sorry,' I tell them.

Mrs. Evans does not look hopeful anymore.

'That's understandable. Don't worry about it. Thank you so much for trying,' Mr. Evans says.

'Yes. Thank you,' Mrs. Evans has tears in her eyes.

'I should probably go now. I'm sorry. Bye,' I get up from the sofa and leave.

'So?' Lucas asks as we walk back to the car.

'Mrs. Evans nearly cried,' I tell him.

'Oh...'.

We get into the car.

'I'm going to go home now,' I tell Lucas.

'Alright,' He says.

Nine

Holly

My house ended up being searched, but nothing was found.
'So are you saying you think Willow is alive?'

'Yes. Have you not thought about that? I think Willow just
don't want to get caught. I think she knew that we were going

to figure out what happened to her, so she tried to scare us off. And it worked,' Ivy tells me.

'But are the police *actually* going to believe your theory?' I ask.

'Probably not, but it's worth a shot,' she says. 'Come on. Let's go,'.

We walk into the police station. Ivy leads me to a front desk, where an officer is standing.

'Hello,' Ivy says.

'Hi, is there anything I can help you with?' the officer asks.

'I have a theory on what happened to Willow Evans,' she says.

'Alright, I'll get Detective Wilson. He was the lead detective in the case,' she smiles.

'Thank you,' Ivy says as the officer walks away.

We go to some dark blue chairs at the wall and sit on them while we wait.

A man who looks as if he's in his mid-fifties walks towards Ivy and I.

'Are you the two girls who had a theory about Willow Evans?' he asks.

He's American. You can tell by the accent.

'Yes,' Ivy says.

'I'm Detective Wilson,' he tells us.

'I'm Ivy. Ivy Greene,'

'Holly Jones,' I say.

'Girls would you two like to come to my office and we can have a little chat about what you've come up with?'.

'Yes, ok,' Ivy says.

We stand up and follow Detective Wilson to a small room.

He gestures for us to sit down on two chairs in front of his desk.

'Alright. What was the theory and how did you come up with it?' he asks.

'So, Holly and I decided to try and solve the case. We didn't get very far. Very little helpful information. We weren't getting anywhere so we gave up about four weeks ago. Today I was thinking if we had made the wrong decision. I don't really know what happened then. I just sort of... started coming up with things that could have happened to Willow,' Ivy explains. We have to lie about why we gave up.

'The theory?'.

'Yes, uhm... I thought that maybe Willow could still be out there somewhere. There's no proof that she's dead. I thought maybe she could be hiding somewhere. She could be scared of something or someone. So scared that she ran away. Maybe she got so used to her new life that she kept livin the same way. Maybe she has some friends somewhere who are helping her stay hidden. Friends that she never told anyone about,' she tells him.

She left out some of that when she was talking to me.

'I like the way you're thinking, Ms. Greene. I'll keep that in mind just in case we come across anything that leads to the case being opened again,' Detective Wilson says. 'But you definitely could come up with more things and write a book. You would make a good author,'.

'Thank you,' she says.

'Is that all you have to say?' he asks us.

'Yes. That's all. Thank you,' I say.

'Alright. Thank you for coming in,'.

'Thank you,' Ivy says.

We walk out of the office and leave the police station.

'What will we do now?' I ask.

'I don't mind,'.

'Should we call Alice and ask her if she wants to do something? Lucas is always with us and so it's never just girls,'.

'Yeah, ok. We should walk back to my house and ask her so she doesn't have to walk by herself,' Ivy tells me.

'Ok,' I say.

We start walking towards Ivy's house. It's not too far from here, so it shouldn't take us long to get there.

'Why do you want Alice to come with us?' Ivy asks.

'I don't know... I just feel like we should ask her. We can have a girls day,'.

'Ok...' Ivy says. She thinks there's a reason why I want Alice to come with us. There's not though.

'No, Ivy. Seriously. There's no actual reason I want Alice to come,'.

We walk up to Ivy's front door. She opens it and we walk inside.

We go upstairs and Ivy knocks on Alice's bedroom door.

'Who is it?' Alice asks.

'It's me,' Ivy tells her.

'Come in,'.

Ivy opens the door. One thing I've noticed is that Ivy locks her door *all* the time. It doesn't matter if she's home or not. The door is *always* locked. But Alice only locks her door when she's changing or sleeping.

'Holly's wondering if you want to have what she calls a *girls day*,'.

'Uhm... ok. Why not,' Alice says. I'm glad she's coming. It'll be more fun with her.

Alice gets up from her bed and picks up a tote bag, similar to the one Ivy always carries. She grabs some money out of a pot on her bedside table and reaches into her bag. She pulls out a wallet. Alice opens the wallet and puts the money from the jar inside it. She drops the wallet back into her bag.

Alice comes out of her room.

'Hi, Holly,' she says.

'Hello,' I reply.

We walk downstairs and leave the house.

•••

We make it into town. We're currently standing right infront of the coffee shop.

'Where will we go first?' Ivy asks.

'I don't mind,' I say. I *do* mind. I want to go dress shopping again.

'Uhm... How about we go get coffee and then we can go book shopping because Ivy likes–sorry, *loves* doing that. Then after that we do something Holly wants to do!' Alice suggests.

'What about you? Shouldn't we do something you want too?' I say.

'Oh... Uh...' Alice is probably thinking of what she wants to do. 'I usually don't get asked what I want to do. Could we go and look at music? Or maybe go to a florist?' she continues.

'Ok. We can do both if you want,' Ivy tells her

'Alright,' Alice smiles.

We turn around and walk inside of the coffee shop.

We walk to the counter.

'Can I get a strawberry frappuccino please,' Alice asks, smiling as she always does.

'Yep. Anything else?' the girl behind the counter asks. I recognise her from school. Oh *God*. It's Valentina. That one girl *everyone* knows. That one girl who is a bitch to everyone. The kind of girl who has a shit load of money. The kiNd of girl who likes Lucas, just because he has money too. The kind of girl you wouldn't expect to be working at a place like this.

The kind of girl who brags about how much money she has. Lucas has money too. But he acts like he doesn't because it's not necessary to brag about money.

Valentina Dalton does *not* like when people call her *Valentina*. Valentina will only answer to *Val*.

'Oh, hi Holly!' Val says, in a cheery voice.

'Hi,' I say.

Val seems to ignore Ivy. Maybe she's figured out that she's Lucas' girlfriend and is jealous of her.

'Could I get an iced tea please,' I ask.

'Yep. Is that it?' Val seems to be getting impatient now.

'Uhm... can I get a caramel latte please,' Ivy finally says something.

'Ok. That's it right? I don't really feel like listening to Ivy Order. I mean– she *did* steal my boyfriend,' Val says. This girl is getting *very* annoying.

'How did my little sister *steal* your boyfriend exactly?' Alice asks in a tone I can't exactly describe.

'She's Lucas White's girlfriend. *I* like Lucas!' she says. She sounds like a little kid arguing over a toy.

'Did you date Lucas before?' Alice asks.

'No, not yet,' Val says in a voice that sort of says *Obviously not are you stupid?*

'Ok, so she *didn't* steal your boyfriend. Let's leave Ivy alone now. Maybe you should get to work, uh, Valentina,' Alice says, glancing at her name tag.

116

'Fine. That will be ten pound, twenty-five pence,' Val says in a bitchy tone.

Alice hands her the exact amount of money.

Val turns around and starts preparing our order.

'I hate her. She's so annoying,' Ivy says.

'Same she's such a—' I'm cut off by Alice playfully hitting me on the shoulder.

'Shut up! She's right there,' Alice whispers.

Val slides our drinks over to us.

'Thank you for deciding to do your job today,' Alice smiles.

We leave the coffee shop before Val can say anything else.

'At one point I thought she was going to start jumping up and down and stomping her feet and throw a tantrum in there,' Ivy says.

We all laugh at that.

I've noticed that Alice likes strawberries a lot. Every time she comes somewhere with Ivy and I, she either orders a strawberry drink or strawberry doughnut or buys something with a strawberry scent or a strawberry printed on it. Her blanket and pillow have little strawberries on them too. It's kind of cute. A seventeen year old girl obsessed with strawberries.

We walk inside the bookshop.

Ivy runs off to look at books. Alice and I Just sort of stand at the door awkwardly for a few seconds.

'Do you want to look around with me?' Alice asks. 'I need a new book. I've read all of the ones I own,'.

It's hard to say no to Alice. She's the kind of girl you just can't resist. You want to do everything you can to make her happy. I don't know how she's still single. She's like a magnet. When you look at her, you just can't take your eyes off her.

'Yeah, why not,' I say.

We start walking around. Ivy is nowhere to be found.

'So... uhm... I don't know what to say. This is kind of awkward if I'm being honest,' Alice says.

'Yeah, *very* awkward,' I reply.

'I don't know how to start a conversation so please don't judge,'.

'You're a little like Ivy in that way,' I say.

'Yeah, I don't know where we got it from though. Our parents are very *outgoing* people,'.

'Oh,'.

'Are you single?' Alice asks. 'Sorry, that was weird,'.

'No, not weird. I am single. Why?'.

'I don't know... I guess I kind of... like you,' she says.

I freeze.

I stop walking.

I don't move.

I wasn't expecting her to say that.

'I know you probably don't feel the same but, you know. What's the point in *wondering* if someone likes you back. Why not just tell them you like them and find out the truth about how they feel about you,'.

'No. I do. I do feel the same,' I say quickly.

'Really?'.

'Yes. What's *not* to like about you, Alice?'.

'I *really* wasn't expecting you to feel the same,'.

I smile.

'I suggested you should come with us today so I could tell you. I got scared so I was having second thoughts. But you said it first, which I wasn't expecting,'.

'So what happens now?' Alice asks.

'I don't know. Do you wanna be my girlfriend?' I ask Alice, hoping for a yes.

'Ok!' she says.

Yes!

'How do we tell Ivy?' I ask.

'Uhm... I don't know. I'll tell her. Ivy knew I liked you and she loved the idea of us being together,' Alice tells me.

'Alright,' I smile.

Alice smiles back.

'Should we look for Ivy? It's been a while and she hasn't come back to us yet,' I ask.

'Yeah, we should,' Alice says.

We walk through the aisles of books. Alice stops and looks at the back of some. She chooses one to buy, so we continue to look for Ivy.

I spot a stack of books and part of Ivy's bag on the floor.

'I think she's over here,' I tell Alice.

We walk towards the pile of books.

There she is. Sitting on the floor reading. She looks so happy when she's in a bookshop. It's like she'd rather be in a bookshop with her head stuck in a book with a coffee beside her than actually experience things.

'Hey!' I say sitting beside her.

'Hi,' she replies, still reading.

Alice sits down too.

'I have to tell you something,' Alice says.

Ivy puts the book down.

'What is it?' she asks.

'Holly and I are uhm... *together,*'

'You mean like... girlfriends?'.

'Yeah, like that,' Alice replies.

'Finally!' Ivy says, seeming relieved. She uses a hand gesture to seem more dramatic. 'Who asked who?'.

'I told Holly I liked her, she asked me to be her girlfriend,'.

'Ahhh!' Ivy says. She doesn't really scream. She just sort of... says it.

'Ok where do you want to go, Holly?' Alice asks.

'Let's go dress shopping!' I say, excitedly.

'Ok,' Alice says.

Alice and Ivy pay for their books and we leave the bookshop.

We cross the road. The clothes shop is right across the road from the bookshop.

We walk into the clothes shop.

It's *really* hot inside.

'You go look around. Ivy and I are going to wait here by the fan,' Alice tells me.

'Ok, I won't be long,' I say.

'Take your time,' Alice smiles.

'No, it's too hot. Give me ten minutes. No longer. Call me if I take any longer. Ok?'.

'Alright,' Ivy says.

I run off into the dress section.

Alice paid for our drinks. I should buy her something.

I spot a nice white dress. I walk over to it to get a closer look.

I check the price

£19.99

I really like it so I pick it up and fold it over my right arm.

I spot a bright pink dress that I really like.

50% OFF!

WAS £19.99

NOW £9.99

It's really cheap so I pick it up and walk over to the top section.

I immediately spot a white puffy-sleeved top with little red and pink strawberries on it. The top reminds me of Alice.

I check the price

£5.99

I put it over my arm with the two dresses.

I spot another top. It's sage green with tiny white flowers and the same puffy sleeves as the one I picked up for Alice.

Ivy.

The top is five pounds ninety-nine.

I put it with the rest of my things. Over my right arm.

I walk to the counter and pay for the dresses and tops. Once I'm done paying, I go back to where Alice and Ivy are.

'I bought yous something each,' I tell them

'You didn't have to!' Alice says, standing up.

'You really didn't,' Ivy says, also standing up.

'Well I did. Let's go,' I say.

We leave the clothes shop. The cold air outside feels nice since it was so hot in there.

'Where are we going next?' Ivy asks.

'Could we look at music?' Alice asks.

'Yeah, ok,' Ivy says.

We walk down the street. The music shop is a few shops down from where we were.

We walk into the music shop.

Alice starts walking around. Ivy and I sit at a shelf of vinyls.

'It's been four weeks since something weird has happened now. I think giving up was a good idea,' Ivy says.

'Yeah. I think so too,'.

About five minutes later, Alice finds us, she's carrying a bag with what I think is four vinyls.

'What did you get?' I ask Alice, as we walk outside.

'I got three vinyls,' she tells me.

I wasn't too far off.

'What are we going to do next? Do you still want to buy flowers?' I ask.

'Yeah, can we?' Alice asks.

'Ok, let's go,' I say.

We start walking towards the local florist, *Violets*. The girl who owns it is named Violet. She once told me that she doesn't even like flowers, and that she just opened a florist because of her name. How stupid does that sound?

Violets is a few minutes away from where we are. So it takes us about ten minutes to walk there.

What are your favourite types of flowers?' I ask Ivy and Alice.

'Uh... Probably peonies. I love the colour. They're *really* pretty,' Alice tells me. 'What's yours Iv?'.

'I don't know. Pansies?'.

'I like them too. They're not my favourite, but I still like them,' Alice says.

'What's your favourite flower, Holly?' Ivy asks.

'Lilacs,' I tell her.

'What do they look like?' Ivy asks.

'Seriously. Do you not know what a *lilac* looks like?'.

'*Seriously*. I don't,'.

I unzip my baby pink bag and take out my phone. I search up *lilacs*.

'*These* are lilacs,' I say, showing Ivy a picture.

'Oh. I've seen them somewhere,' she tells me.

'I'm not surprised you have. They're pretty popular,' Alice says.

We finally get to Violets.

We walk inside. It smells nice here. There are lots of pretty flowers. Roses. Lilies. Carnations.

Alice spots her favourite flowers. She picks up a bouquet of peonies.

I walk around, admiring all of the flowers.

I don't think Ivy really likes flowers. She prefers plants. Like, green ones. The boring ones.

I think it's kind of funny the way she has fake ivy hanging on one of her bedroom walls. I mean– her name *is* Ivy and she has *ivy* on her wall. I don't think that was a very funny joke.

Ivy has some plants in her room. Most of them are real. She looks after them quite well too.

I find some lilacs. I pick up a small bouquet of them.

124

I think I like one of the most *basic* flowers *ever*.

'Have you found anything you want to buy?' I ask Ivy, who is now standing right beside me.

'No. I don't think I need flowers. They're expensive and I'll probably just end up letting them die,' she says.

'But you have plants in your room. They can't be much different to flowers,'.

'I know. I'll forget about the flowers. Every time Alice buys me flowers I *forget* about them and they just... die,'.

'Ok then,'.

I walk to the counter to pay. I hand Violet money. Violet gives me the change.

Alice is already waiting at the door.

Ivy and I walk to the door and we all leave the shop.

Ten

Ivy

I got a text this morning.

A text from *?*.

I thought it was over but it clearly isn't.

I pick up my phone and text Lucas and Holly

Me: Can you both come to my house? I have to tell you something.

Holly: Yep be right there

Lucas: Gimme 5 mins :)

Me: Thanks.

Once they both get here I'm going to tell Alice to come into my room too. I'm going to show them all the text.

I'm scared. I'm *really* scared.

Someone is still stalking me. I'm not sure about Holly.

I got the letter five weeks ago now. That's over a month ago. But I can't stop thinking about it. I just want to know *who* sent it. Or maybe just a hint. But I know they won't tell me. What kind of stalker tells the people they're stalking that they're stalking them? None that *I* have heard of, anyways.

Holly: abt to walk in now cya in 2 seconds

Me: ok

Lucas: almost there :D

Me: :D

  'Hey! What were you wanting to tell us?' Holly asks,
opening my room door. 'And why isn't your door locked?'.
'I'll tell you when Lucas gets here. I'm also going to ask Alice
to come in. And I forgot to lock it when my mum left my
room,'.

'Ok,'.

  About five minutes later, someone knocks on the front
door.

  My mum opens the door.

'Ivy! Your boyfriend whose name I keep forgetting is here!'
she

calls.

'Tell him to come up. Holly's here!' I call back.

  Lucas walks up the stairs and into my room.

'Should I close the door?' he asks.

'No. I'm going to get Alice,'.

'Alright,' he says, sitting on my bed beside me.

  I stand up and walk out of my bedroom. I knock on Alice's
door.

  'Yeah?'.

'Can you come into my room for a minute? I have to show
you, Holly and Lucas something,'.

'Ok, just a second!,'.

When Alice says a second, she *literally* means a second, because a second later she comes out of her room.

We walk into my room. I lock my door. I sit beside Lucas. Alice and Holly are sitting on the floor.

I hear my parents leave the house.

I pick up my phone and go to my camera roll to find the screenshot I took of the text.

I find the picture.

'I got this text this morning,' I say, showing Alice and Holly first then turning the phone to Lucas.

The text says *Did you really think giving up would stop me?*

'You should have told us sooner!' Lucas says.

'I know... sorry,'.

'Don't apologise. But you should have at least told Alice when you got it,' he tells me.

'Yeah, I should have,'.

Neither of the two girls say anything. They look shocked.

I turn to look at Lucas. He's staring blankly out my window. I look out the window too and realise why he's staring out the window.

There is someone dressed from head to toe in black standing in front of my house.

'Holly, Alice. Look. Outside. Right. Now,' I say.

'Why?' Holly asks.

'Just look!' Lucas says.

Holly and Alice both stand up and look outside. They turn back, looking as if they just saw a ghost. It's not a ghost they saw. I don't think it is anyways. No. It can't be a ghost.

Ghosts. Do. Not. Exist.

'Let's go outside,' Holly says.

'What? No!' Alice looks at Holly like she's a psychopath.

'Ok. I'll go with you,' I tell Holly.

'No, please don't, Ivy,' Lucas says.

'I'm going,' I say.

They're not going to stop me.

I stand up and give Lucas a hug.

'I'll be fine,' I tell him.

'Are you sure?' he asks.

'Yes. I'm sure,'.

'Ok. I'll watch from the window,' Lucas tells me.

'I will too,' Alice says.

'Bye,' Holly says.

I unlock my door. We leave my room and go downstairs. We go outside

'Why are you outside my house?' I ask.

'Ivy. It's lovely to finally meet you,' The person says. It sounds like a girl's voice. 'Holly. I believe we've met,'.

'Uh... I don't know. Are you the person who shot me?'.

'Yes,'.

'Why are you doing this?' I ask.

'Because it's fun!'.

This person needs help. I mean this in a serious way. They're stalking sixteen year olds.

'Why did you choose *us* though?' Holly asks.

'Because you're easy targets,'.

'I have to go to the bathroom. I'll be back,' Holly says.

She doesn't give me a chance to say anything. She just goes inside.

I feel sick.

Holly

I run upstairs and into Ivy's room.

'Why did you leave her by herself?' Lucas asks, panicked.

'I'm going to the bathroom. She'll be fine,' I tell them.

I leave the room and walk into the upstairs bathroom.

I just stand there and try to process what's happening.

I probably shouldn't have left Ivy by herself, but I'm sure she'll be fine. Right?

'Holly!' Alice shouts.

I run out of the bathroom and back into Ivy's room.

'What?'.

'Ivy... gone,' she says,

'What do you mean she's *gone*?'.

'She's not there. Neither is that weird person...' she tells me.

Lucas looks terrified.

I feel like I'm the worst person in the whole world.

Ivy is *missing* because of me.

'No...' I say. 'Shit. It's all my fault!' I start to cry.

'It's not your fault,' Alice says.

'Yes it is. I left her. I'm the worst friend ever,' I sob.

Alice walks over to me and wraps her arms around me.

'I'm sorry,' I say. I really mean it. I feel so stupid.

'It's ok,' Alice starts to cry too.

Alice and I sit on Ivy's bed. Lucas sits with us.

'She can't be gone too far. Can she?' he says.

'I don't know. I don't even know who the person who took her is,' I find it hard to say anything. It's hard to accept that your best friend is gone.

I start crying even harder.

'Let's go outside and look for her,' Lucas says.

'Ok,' I whisper.

We all stand up, leave Ivy's room, go downstairs and we go outside.

'IVY!' Alice calls. 'IVY! WHERE ARE YOU?'.

'IVY!' Lucas shouts.

'Ivy?' I attempt to shout too, but my voice is too weak so it comes out quietly.

I spot Ivy and Alice's parents' car at the top of the street.

'There's your parents,' I tell Alice.

'Let's go back inside. We can explain everything to them. The texts, calls, the person,' Alice says.

'Ok,' Lucas replies.

We go back inside and go back to Ivy's room.

Ivy and Alice's parents open the front door.

'Ivy! Alice! Are you home?' their dad asks.

They must not have seen us outside.

Nobody answers him.

He walks upstairs and comes into Ivy's room.

'Where's Ivy?' he asks.

'We don't know,' Lucas tells him.

'What do you mean you don't know?'.

'Ivy and Holly went outside and Holly came inside to use the bathroom. Alice and I were watching them from the window. Alice looked out and Ivy was gone. She's not here,'.

'What's going on?' Ivy's mum asks, walking up the stairs.

'Ivy is missing,' her dad says.

'What? No. She can't be!'.

'I'm sorry,' I say again.

'Why are you sorry, Holly?' Mrs. Greene asks.

'I came inside to use the bathroom and Alice called me and said she was missing. She's nowhere to be found,' I tell her.

'Why did you go outside?' Mr. Greene asks.

'We saw a person dressed in all black outside. Ivy and I were being stalked and Ivy got another text for the first time in five weeks this morning. That's why Lucas and I are here. She wanted to show us. I've seen the person before. They came to my door once. They also shot me. I shouldn't have left her by herself. I wasn't thinking straight. I was scared they'd pull out a gun again. I'm sorry,' I explain.

Alice hugs me again.

Lucas looks empty.

Alice is still crying. So am I.

'I'm going to call 999 and report her missing,' Mrs. Greene tells us

'Ok,' Alice says quietly.

Ivy and Alice's mum takes her phone out of her pocket and dials 999.

'My daughter is missing,' She says.

'Her name is Ivy Greene. She is sixteen. She has light brown hair, blue eyes. She was last seen wearing a sage green top with white flowers, puffy sleeves and black baggy jeans,'.

I spot a tear stream down Lucas' face.

'Yes. It's out of character. Her best friend, her boyfriend and her older sister told me and my husband that they saw a person dressed in all black outside of the house. She went missing from my house. She lives with me and her father,'.

Mrs. Greene proceeds to tell the police the address.

'Thank you so much. Goodbye,' Mrs Greene hangs up the phone. 'The police are on their way over. You're all going to be interviewed,' she tells us.

'I was expecting that. They always interview friends,' I say.

Lucas is still silent.

About five minutes later, police are knocking on the door.

Mr. Greene answers it.

The police come straight upstairs and ask Alice, Lucas and I to leave Ivy's room so they can search it.

Another officer takes me to the back garden so I can be interviewed. I'm not nervous. I know I didn't do anything to Ivy. I *did* leave her outside on her own.

'Ok. What's your name?' the officer asks.

'Holly Jones,'.

'Age?'.

'Sixteen,'.

'What would you say you are to Ivy?'.

'We're best friends,'.

'When did you last see Ivy?'.

'When we were out the front,'.

'And what happened exactly?'.

'We saw someone outside dressed in all black. Ivy and I decided to go outside to see who it was. I needed to use the bathroom so I went inside. Her sister Alice and my other best friend Lucas were watching us from Ivy's bedroom window, so I thought Ivy would be fine for a minute by herself. I was wrong. I was in the bathroom and Alice shouted to me that Ivy was gone. She and Lucas had looked away for a second and Alice looked back outside and Ivy was nowhere to be seen. Lucas, her boyfriend, suggested we go outside and look. We did exactly that. We were calling for her. I spotted Alice and Ivy's parents' car at the top of the street so I told Alice. Alice then suggested we go inside and tell them everything. About Ivy and I getting texts and calls from someone going by the name *question mark* and about the person.We went inside and back to Ivy's room. Her parents came inside. They didn't see us outside. Her dad shouted upstairs asking if Alice and Ivy were home. Nobody said anything. He came upstairs and into Ivy's room. He asked where Ivy was. Lucas told him that we didn't know. He explained that she was missing then Mrs. Greene came upstairs. I explained everything then she called and reported Ivy missing,' I explain.

'Alright, thank you,' the officer says. 'You can go inside,'.

I go inside to the living room, where Lucas and Alice are. I sit on the sofa beside Alice.

The same police officer who interviewed me comes into the living room behind me and asks for Alice.

Ivy

Black. All I see is black. I don't know where I am. My phone is in my bag. I think I still have my bag on my shoulder but I don't know.

I reach over and my bag is there. I put my arm in and find my phone.

I turn it on. There's no signal.

Shit.

I go to *emergency* and dial 999.

It won't work.

Shit.

I don't know what to do.

Eleven

Holly

A WEEK LATER

It's been a week since Ivy went missing.

She still hasn't been found.

I wonder if she's even still *alive*.

The past week has been nothing but interviews and police.

I just want to know if she's ok.

The police said they will find Ivy. They said they won't give up. Well that's good to know because if it was *me* trying to find her, I would *definitely* fail.

Ivy

I was stabbed yesterday.

I think I've been gone for about a week now.

I just want to go home.

'Ivy?' the person says.

I say nothing.

'Ivy, I don't think you're going to go home. I think it's time I reveal my identity,' they walk into my dark room. 'I'm your sister,'.

'What? Alice wouldn't do this,'.

'I'm not Alice. I'm your *other* sister,' they laugh.

'I don't have another sister...' I say, slowly.

'Of course you do!'.

A light flickers on.

Willow Evans.

Willow Evans is standing before me.

'You're not my sister,'.

'Yes I am,'.

'How?'

'Your parents had me when they were young. They didn't
have the money to raise a child, so they put me up for
adoption. My parents told me that the day before I ran away.
They didn't tell anyone I was adopted. They somehow got
away with a fake birth certificate. I wanted to meet my real
parents, but my adoptive parents wouldn't allow it. I did
threaten to run away a few times, but I never did, so when I
said I would that last time, they didn't believe me, but what
did I do? I ran away. I wanted to punish my totally real
parents, so I ran away. I ended up liking being here, so I
stayed. I found out that I had a little sister, who was born a
year after I was. So our parents couldn't afford to raise me
but could afford to raise another child a year later? That's
stupid,' Willow says.

'But why did you kidnap me?' I ask.

'I kidnapped you because I'm jealous of you and I want the
perfect friend and perfect boyfriend and perfect life. I want to
be you so badly, Ivy. You don't *understand*. I want a life with
my *real* family and friends who are actually *nice* to me and a
rich boyfriend who could buy me anything I want,'.

'Why me and not Alice?'.

'I don't want to be Alice. I want to be *you*. Are you listening
to what I'm saying?'.

'Yes,' I say.

'Good,'.

  I close my eyes.

I can't believe what is happening right now.

I feel like I'm dreaming.

'But why Holly too?'.

'Holly was trying to solve the case with you and I didn't want to be caught so I decided to try and scare you both off. Then I found out that you were my youngest sister. I wanted to take you. I wanted to know what your life is like so I decided to take the opportunity to kidnap you last week. Oh and by the ,' she explains.

'Why did you stab me?' I ask.

'I was bored last night and I had a knife on me so I stabbed you. I stab things a lot. I also shoot the walls when I'm bored of stabbing things. I was excited when I got to stab a real person,'.

I think Willow is a little out of her mind.

'Why do you stab and shoot things?'.

'Because it's fun. I think I might have stabbed myself in my sleep once or twice,'.

'Oh...' I don't really know what I'm supposed to say to that. 'How about we both leave here and go home. You can meet our parents and I'll make up a story and lie for you so you don't get in trouble!' I suggest.

'What story?'.

'I'll say that I overheard my parents talking about you being my sister so I went to find you because you called me and told me where you were. I found you and brought you home.

The person in black just left and they didn't do anything wrong,'.

'Ok. Fine. We can do that. If you tell the truth I will shoot you in the head and kill you,' Willow turns on a light.

She still has the same long black hair. She has a scar going across the bottom of her nose. She looks sort of like me. She has my dad's green eyes. Alice does too. I can see that she is my older sister.

'Are you ready to meet the rest of your family?'

Twelve

Holly

I'm sitting in my room. My little sister Harper is begging me to play with her. I *really* don't want to. Ivy is still missing. I just want to see her again. I miss her more than I thought I could ever miss someone.

'Please, Holly! *Please* play with me!' Harper begs.

'Harper, I don't really feel like playing,'.

'Why?'.

'I'm busy thinking about Ivy,' I tell her.

'Ok,' she folds her arms and stomps out of my room.

I get a notification on my phone. I pick it up and turn it on.

It's from the group with Ivy, Lucas and I.

Ivy: I'm on my way home.

Lucas: IVY OML ARE YOU OK?

Ivy: Yes, I'm ok.

Me: OMG IVY HI

I call 999 right after I reply to Ivy.

999: What's your emergency?

Me: I have something on the Ivy Greene case.

999: What is it?

Me: She texted me and her boyfriend Lucas in a group.

999: And what's your name?

Me: Holly Jones.

999: Ok, Holly. Call back if you have any more information. Thank you.

Me: Thanks, bye.

I put my phone into my handbag and run out of the room, down the stairs and out the door. I don't tell anyone where I'm going.

I run as fast as I possibly can to Ivy and Alice's house.

I finally get there and I open the door as I usually do without knocking.

'Holly?' Alice shouts

I run upstairs and into Alice's room.

'I got a text from Ivy!' I say.

'What?'.

I pull out my phone and show Alice the text.

'Oh my God,' she says, in shock.

'Are your parents home?' I ask.

'No. I'll text them,'.

A few minutes pass. Mr. and Mrs. Greene don't see the text.

Alice and I are sitting on the step outside the front door.

Lucas got here a few minutes ago. He's standing behind us.

A black jeep pulls up into the driveway.

Ivy gets out.

She runs over to Alice and hugs her. Then she hugs me.

'Oh my God. I missed you so much!' I say.

'I missed you too!' Ivy replies.

'Where were you? What happened? Lucas asks as Ivy pulls away from me and moves to him.

'I overheard our parents saying that Willow Evans was our sister. She was adopted. She ran away because her parents wouldn't let her meet her real parents. She wanted to punish her parents. Willow ended up liking being alone so she stayed. There's a lot of explaining. Willow will explain later,' she says, looking at Alice. 'She texted me and told me where she was so I went looking for her. I found her. We spent a week getting to know each other. She's in the car now,'.

Ivy sits on the doorstep.

'I'm not leaving again. I promise,'.

Ivy and Alice's parents' car pulls up into the driveway, next to the black jeep.

Ivy

I jump up from the doorstep. Mum and dad get out of the car.

I run over to them

'Hi!' I say.

'What happened? Are you ok?' My mum asks.

'I found Willow. My sister,' I say.

'What?'.

'I know that she was adopted. I overheard you and dad saying she was my sister,' I lie.

I hate lying to everyone. I just don't want to die.

We all go inside. Including Willow.

Willow and I tell everyone the story I made up.

Everyone seems to believe it.

'So you weren't kidnapped?' Lucas asks.

'No. I wasn't,' I lie.

'Ok,'.

My dad called 999 and told them that everything is ok and that I'm home.

My mum called Willow's adoptive parents and told them that Willow is safe.

I'm home.

Willow is home.

Everybody is happy again.

The End

Authors Note

This is the first ever book I've written. I'm proud of myself as I'm only twelve.

Thank you for taking the time to read my book. It means so much to me that you decided to read the book I've written out of all the books in the world.

I probably wouldn't have written this if I didn't read. I only read because my best friend took my money and bought the book I was too scared to buy. That was April 20th 2022. Ever since then I've been addicted to reading, thanks to my best friend.

I'd like to say thanks to my mam. We were in the car one day and I said 'I want to write a book when I'm older' and my mam said 'Don't wait until you're older. You should try now'. I did exactly that. I wrote this.

And thank you to my dad, who gave me the idea for the phone call from the party scene.

I would laugh at the first five chapters, but I want to leave them because it shows that I've made progress.

Emily

Printed in Great Britain
by Amazon

14039948R00089